Tempt Him

Tempt Him

**The Man Trap Series
Book One**

By

OLIVIA JAYMES

www.OliviaJaymes.com

TEMPT HIM
Copyright © 2018 by Olivia Jaymes
Print Edition

Tempt Him

I'm Mia and I've been in love with Joshua Henry for as long as I can remember. Since the day he picked me up off the sidewalk after I fell off of my bike, I haven't been able to see anyone but him.

Unfortunately, Josh sees me as the sweet girl from next door, not a romantic partner. I'm stuck in the friend zone and there isn't an exit in sight.

But now everything has changed. After a near death experience, I'm a different woman. The kind of female that doesn't sit back and wait. I'm going after what I want, and what I want is Josh Henry.

My sister Shelby – the psychological genius – has written a how-to manual to help me. It's the perfect blueprint to make the perfect man fall in love with me.

I'm setting a man trap… and I'm doing it by the book. Care to join me?

CHAPTER ONE

Mia

I WAS LATE again. It wasn't unusual and my friends were used to it. For all I knew, they had told me a meeting time fifteen minutes early so I wouldn't be tardy. It wasn't that I didn't want to be punctual. I did. It simply never seemed to work out. I was born at forty-two weeks and have been running late ever since. A fact my mother hasn't let me forget in all of my thirty-one years. As far as she is concerned, I ruined Christmas and New Year's.

Take today, for example, this was an outing I'd been looking forward to all week. I don't get to spend near enough time with my friends these days and we'd planned a long, leisurely lunch in one of the trendy bistros in the downtown area. I was planning to blow a weekend's worth of calories on dessert alone. The chocolate cake was already calling my name.

I had dressed in plenty of time but then my neighbor stopped me on the way to my car to talk about how I felt about the new sidewalks they were putting in. Was I for or against? Which is why I was jogging down the sidewalk in my lime green Converse tennis shoes and sweating in my white cotton sweater and denim jacket.

It was autumn and there was a definite nip in the air. Fall

was my absolute favorite season. Even in a little university town like Arborville – smack dab in the middle of corn and cows – there was charm. The leaves were beginning to turn and thoughts of summer fun were fading quickly.

I made my rushed apologies to my sister Shelby and our friends Emmy and Ashlyn. I wasn't sure just how long we'd all been friends or how we all became a group, but of course Shelby and I were sisters, so we were sort of forced to be friends. Shelby and Mia Kelly, the two redheaded girls on the block. We'd taken a lot of shit about our hair color.

Shelby and I met Ashlyn in a yoga class years ago and Ashlyn and Emmy have been friends since childhood. Somehow that translated into our tight-knit little quartet of cozy estrogen.

My friends had ordered me an iced tea which I gratefully gulped after sitting down.

"We knew you'd be late, Mia," Shelby said with a roll of her eyes that would have made a teenage girl proud. "But now that you're here I can tell everyone my amazing news."

"News?" I parroted. What other news could she have? She'd already announced her engagement a few months ago. Was she pregnant, too?

My sister reached into that oversized handbag like Mary Poppins and pulled out a three-ring binder. "This is it. I finished it."

"It?" I wasn't sure what she was talking about. Shelby was always talking. I couldn't remember every single thing she'd ever said. I wouldn't have room in my brain for things like weather and which fork to use.

"My book," she said excitedly, flipping open the plastic pink cover. She was practically vibrating in the chair. "I finished my book. The one about relationships and finding the right man."

I leaned over and scanned the title page.

How to Trap a Man by Dr. Shelby Kelly.

I looked up at my sister in disbelief. "A man trap? It sounds…archaic. And misogynistic."

"It's supposed to be a fun title, not serious. I guess it could change." She had a pleading look on her face that usually melted any resistance. With other people, but not me. "C'mon, you all swore you'd help me if I ever finished. Well, I've finished. Now I need testers for the assignments that I give the readers."

No way. We had no way of knowing when we'd made that agreement that Shelby would ever finish. In fact, I was pretty sure we were all counting on her being far too busy to ever complete an entire book.

"I know what happened to your last guinea pig. He's buried under Mom's rose bushes."

Shelby huffed her disapproval. "He died of old age. It was nothing I did."

"Old age? He lived with us for six months. Hardly a geriatric."

"He was old when I got him. So you're not going to help me? Even though you promised? I can't believe this. I think I need new friends. I completed the biggest project of my entire life and this is the response I get? I'm disgusted with all of you."

We weren't being very nice but everyone sitting at that table knew what was going to happen. We were all going to say no and then Shelby was going to mention it every time we were together until one by one we all gave in. I was convinced that my sister enjoyed the dance and that if we all just said yes, she'd be slightly let down.

I lifted my iced tea and took a dainty sip, studiously avoiding her gaze. "I'm very busy right now. Maybe in a few months. I'm kind of off men at the moment."

I could feel the weight of my older sister's stare. She was bossy and it made me crazy. My life wasn't exactly perfect but hers? Practically a fairytale. She had a PhD in psychology. She taught part time at the local junior college, had a thriving private practice, was working on a book, did Pilates, cooked like a gourmet, and had a handsome and successful fiancé that she'd met five years ago at a wine tasting event for charity. Yep, wine tasting.

See? Perfect. I was surrounded and couldn't escape. Right now that annoying big sister was about to say something that we would both regret. I could feel it coming but I couldn't stop it.

"Are you still in love with him?"

Shelby had cut straight to the heart of the matter. No beating around the bush.

"Does it matter?"

"Yes. Are you?"

The other girls had fallen silent. No one was going to rescue me. They all knew who Shelby was talking about.

The one man that I'd been avoiding for the last month.

Joshua Henry.

He'd lived in the house next door to ours when I was growing up. Five years older and always and forever out of my league. Tall and sexy, with dark curly hair that always seemed to need a trim, he was my dream man. And by dream man I mean that the only way I'd ever be getting him was in my dreams.

Over the years we'd fallen into a friendship of sorts and we hanged out quite a bit. But to save my sanity, I'd stopped returning his calls and texts. I'd even stopped frequenting the places I knew he'd be. It was a drastic step, but I'd had to do it for my own sake. A woman can only take so much.

"We should order." I picked up my menu and buried my nose in it which was ridiculous. We all knew the menu by heart. "I think I might try the risotto."

"You hate risotto," Shelby said. "Now answer the question."

"I'm not one of your patients, Shel. I am your sister." I pulled the menu down so I could look her in the eye. "And I could like risotto. Maybe I've tried it and loved it."

"Have you?"

"You're annoying."

"In other words, no. So do you still love him? It's okay if you do."

My sister was like a dog with a bone and she wasn't going to shut the hell up until I answered. Honestly.

"Yes, can we order now?"

Ashlyn, the soft-hearted one in the group, immediately reached across the table and grabbed my hand. "Oh honey, I'm so sorry. Unrequited love is awful."

I shrugged, not wanting to make this a bigger deal than it already was. "It's fine. He keeps calling and I keep ignoring him."

Shelby turned to the other two women. "She's been in love with him since we were kids."

That was true, although I don't know why she was saying it.

Ashlyn and Emmy already knew. Everybody knew except Josh. The big bonehead.

"I fell off my bicycle and he helped me up. I'd scraped my knee."

For me it had been a magical moment. Josh lifting me up in his strong arms. I had been about eight and he'd been a mature thirteen, practically a grown man in my eyes. I wasn't sure why I was repeating the story because they'd heard it all before during a drunken night watching chick flicks where I had decided that I'd had enough watching Josh date other women. It was that night that I'd found something of a backbone and not returned his latest text. Or any of the ones after. You would think it would have gotten easier after awhile but it hadn't. I missed him and thought about him far more than I should.

"And love began," Emmy replied in a sour tone. She was the cynical one of our group. "That man has been nothing but trouble for you. I am in full support of you not returning any of his calls. You need to find a new man, a better one."

The waitress had had enough of their stalling. With toe tapping impatience, she planted herself at Shelby's elbow, her pencil posed to take their order. It was always the same.

Emmy didn't have to worry about her weight because she was constantly on the run with her job as an event planner and burned calories like a squirrel on Red Bull. Frankly, I think calories are terrified of Emmy. They won't come anywhere near her. She ordered the double cheeseburger and fries with a side of cholesterol medicine.

Ashlyn, like myself, constantly battled the scale and we both liked dessert. She ordered the grilled chicken sandwich with the special sauce on the side. As the owner of the coolest retro shop in town, she didn't get a chance to work out as much as she'd like to.

Shelby never worried about anything in her life, convinced it would all work out for the best, so she ordered chicken smothered in cheese and mushrooms along with a baked potato. Butter only, because she said sour cream just sounded like it didn't taste good. I wasn't sure if she was aware that it was in cheesecake but I wasn't going to be the one to tell her.

I ordered the chicken stir-fry but I was absolutely having the dark chocolate cake afterward. I wasn't going to share it, either. I had a fork and I wasn't afraid to use it as a weapon.

The waitress headed back to the kitchen and Shelby clasped her hands together, smiling widely. "Emmy, I think you have a fabulous idea. We need to find Mia a new guy. We can use the book to do it."

We all groaned simultaneously. People in happy relationships always think it's so easy to find a mate, but it's not. Considering the last several dates I'd been on I was beginning to think it was downright impossible.

I was not going to be railroaded into road testing Shelby's ridiculous book. I couldn't even look at it without cringing. Man trap. What self-respecting woman would trap a man? Not me.

"No. You'll need to find another victim. Oops, I mean volunteer."

Shelby snapped the binder closed. "Do you remember that party you threw your senior year of high school? The one when Mom and Dad were visiting Nana? You know…the one I never told them about?"

I narrowed my eyes and gave my sister the meanest look I could. She was playing dirty pool.

"Is that a threat?"

Shelby's fingers drummed on the table. "I'm not making any threats. I'm just saying that I never told Mom and Dad."

Because my sister had been holding onto that for this very moment. I wouldn't forget this. This wasn't our usual game of me saying no and then finally saying yes at some point down the road. Shelby was playing in the big leagues when it came to this book.

"I'm an adult now. It doesn't matter."

"Then it won't matter if I tell them. Will it?"

She thought I would fold like a cheap tent. She was going to be disappointed. I was going to be gracious and happy for my sister even though she was a low-down dirty dog for trying to blackmail me. Two could play that game. She had secrets too, and as the little sister I'd spent many years cataloguing every one of them. She had no idea who she was dealing with. I'd kept my eyes open and I knew stuff. Big stuff.

"It won't matter at all. By the way, did you ever tell Mom and Dad about that night at the drive-in with Steve Baker? It was such a great story. Now shouldn't we have a toast and celebrate your book?"

I really did feel that we should celebrate even when Shelby annoyed the hell out of me. She was amazing and I loved her. But I wasn't going to be forced to humiliate myself with men just so my sister could rack up another accomplishment on her long and prestigious resume.

At least not right away. She was going to have to work for it, and since she'd brought up that party, I wouldn't mind some begging and groveling, too.

I was far too busy avoiding Josh to spend time finding another man.

CHAPTER TWO

Josh

I WAS FEEDING the parking meter in the downtown area when my phone went off. I was supposed to be meeting a woman I'd been dating for a few months for lunch. I'd been busting my ass all week and I planned to have some fun this weekend and relax. Running my own business was great but sometimes it could become all-consuming. I needed to slow down every now and then, but I never seemed to.

"What do you want, Luke?"

Luke was my younger brother by eighteen months and also my best friend when he wasn't being an ass. After hating corporate America, he'd come to work with me at my video game design business about two years ago. Working with family always made for an interesting and often frustrating workday but he did a damn good job of keeping all the numbers straight. I hated numbers.

"I want to know why I'm in the office today and you aren't."

"Because I'm the boss?"

That wasn't going to work with Luke.

"Whatever. Seriously, you have a deadline looming and you're cool as a cucumber. Did you stay up every night all week and get the storyline done? Have you been hiding that from me?"

The storyline. The first part of my game design and the bedrock that the interface rested on. If it wasn't right, no cool graphics could save it.

"I'll get it done."

I could hear Luke's exasperated sigh in my ear. I wasn't all that happy about it either, but that's why I was taking some time off. I needed to recharge my creative batteries.

"Has Mia called you back?"

No, and that was unusual. She might show up everywhere fifteen minutes late but she was excellent about returning calls. However, I'd left over a dozen messages and she hadn't returned one of them. I'd started checking the local paper to make sure she hadn't shown up in the obituaries.

Mia had always been a sweet kid growing up next to me and my parents. Funny and interesting to talk to. With her red hair and freckles she was teased by some of the neighborhood kids and those big glasses she always wore didn't help things. Or the fact that she always had her nose stuck in a book. It was all that reading though that made her so fun to talk to. She seemed to know something about everything and she knew a hell of a lot about history. That's why I needed her help. My new video game was set in the Roaring Twenties and I needed her expertise.

"Not yet. I'll send her another message. If she doesn't return this one, I'll call her sister Shelby. I hope Mia isn't sick or hurt."

I was positive that if something really bad had happened I would have heard about it from my mom and dad who still lived next to Mia's parents. I think my mom and her mom had coffee together just about every morning, rain or shine.

"Maybe she's got a boyfriend and he's keeping her busy."

"She doesn't have a boyfriend."

"How do you know?" Luke reasoned. "She could have a boyfriend. She's pretty with all that red hair and freckles. Some guys drool over that."

"I'm not one of them."

There was a moment of silence and then Luke chuckled. "Never said you were, bro. Just that some men really dig that. Anyway, call her again. You need her help badly."

I did, actually. I needed her to go into detail about the time period and tell me all sorts of stories about the people that no one ever learned in school. She always inspired me when I was creating a game, and I only had to pay her in pizza and chocolate.

"You shouldn't be talking about Mia that way. Shit, she's like our little sister."

"Except that she's not," Luke shot back. "We're not related in any way and I happened to notice that she grew into a hottie. I may be married but I am allowed to look. Mia is easy on the eyes."

I'd never thought about Mia's looks. She was much more than the sum of her lady parts, if you know what I mean. She wasn't a typical female in my experience. She didn't go in for all the giggling and games other women played. Straightforward and honest. That was my Mia.

"Did I say fuck you? Because I meant to."

"You did."

"So shut up."

"I'm not saying a word."

"Good. Don't."

"But she is hot."

I didn't like him talking about Mia. At all. It felt wrong about ten different ways.

"Fuck you."

"You said that."

"I meant it. Now I'm at the restaurant and I'm meeting Trisha for lunch so get back to work."

I did hang up without another word but then I sent another text. To Mia. One more try. If she didn't answer this one, I'd show up at her front door.

★　★　★

Mia

I'D MANAGED TO leave lunch and make it home without committing to help test my sister's new book. Shelby had made a few vague threats but she had to be aware that I had just as much dirt on her as she had on me. If she wanted my help – and our friends' help – she needed to make it worth our while. Perhaps she could let us pick out the bridesmaid dresses so we all didn't resemble a feather duster like my cousin Sandy at *her* sister's nuptials.

The theme of the wedding had been birds. That's right...birds. They were everywhere. On top of the cake, in the bouquet, on the tuxedo lapels of the men. They even hung from the ceiling looking like a scene from that Alfred Hitchcock film. They only thing missing was a phone booth for Sandy to hide in.

I had a stack of quizzes to grade, so I changed clothes so I could curl up and be comfortable. It was a rainy afternoon and perfect weather for hanging around the house. I was halfway through the stack and a glass of Chardonnay when I heard a knock on my front door. It was probably one of the kids from the neighborhood telling me that their Frisbee had landed on my roof. Despite the lousy weather, they'd been playing out in the street when I came home. I lived in a cul de sac of a small condo community and we didn't get much traffic back here. They were going to have to wait to get it back because I wasn't going to climb on top of my house after even a half a glass of wine. They weren't going to do it either as I was fairly sure my homeowner's insurance wouldn't like that.

I swung open the door and froze, my words of greeting dying in my throat. It wasn't the neighbor kids standing on my doorstep.

Shit and double shit.

It was Josh Henry, looking better than he had a right to. Asshole. Well-washed denim that looked like it was made just for him, a white button-down shirt, and a soft as butter brown leather jacket. He could have stepped out of a magazine and I wanted to stomp on his toes for just standing there on my front porch. He had some nerve walking around looking like that, especially when I looked like something the cat had dragged in. Or thrown up on the carpet.

Ragged sweats, a holey t-shirt with my alma mater splattered across unfettered boobs, and my long hair pulled up in a ponytail so it was off my face while I worked. If I stood out on the street like this, people would put spare change in my coffee cup. The only thing I currently had going for me was that I hadn't washed off the makeup I'd worn to lunch. If my mascara wasn't under my eyes, at least my face looked presentable.

Self-consciously, I touched the ends of my auburn hair. I normally kept the curls short but had decided to give long hair a try at the urging of my sister. She too had inherited the Irish coloring of our mother, pale skin and reddish hair, although hers was a shade darker than mine. She also didn't get the freckles that I'd been blessed – or cursed – with but we did have matching green eyes. I was, however, two inches shorter than Shelby, which I put down to my mother giving up on eating a healthy diet with her second child. With the first she'd been super vigilant. With me she'd eaten entire pies in one sitting. I'd heard stories from my aunts.

"Josh." I glanced nervously from side to side, not wanting to be dazzled by his looks. I needed to keep my head on straight during this encounter, but I'd already noticed that his hair was slightly wet from the rain. It curled even more when it was wet. "How–how are you?"

He smiled, showing off even white teeth that had never needed braces. Of course not. He was perfect, after all. "I'm good. How are you? I haven't seen you in forever."

I scrambled for an explanation as to why I'd suddenly disappeared off the face of the earth, but sadly I wasn't that smart or quick or creative. I settled for boring.

"Busy. I've been busy. You know how it is."

He nodded as if he understood. "I do. Work has been crazy, but I wouldn't have it any other way. You must have just started a new school year."

I teach at John Adams High School. Ms. Mia Kelly, history teacher. Nice to meet you.

"About a month ago, yes. It's good. The kids are great. We're doing the Revolutionary War right now."

His smile widened and his eyes twinkled. He looked so yummy. I hated him right now. "Your favorite war."

We were standing in my doorway and it was becoming awkward. He obviously was here to talk and not out on the porch. "It is."

This time he seemed to pick up on my straying thoughts, his own gaze looking over my shoulder.

"Can I come in? Do you have company?"

Company? What? He thought my reluctance was because I already had a guest? Did I look like I was having a wild party in here?

I shook my head. "No, no one else is here. I was just grading papers. Come on in. Do you want a glass of wine or something else? I can make coffee."

Shrugging off his damp jacket, he draped it on the closet door knob so if it dripped it would do it on my foyer tile. He settled onto my overstuffed couch and picked up my wine glass while I hovered nervously nearby. Josh had been over to my house a million times but suddenly I wasn't sure how to deal with it. I didn't want him here. "A little early, isn't it?"

I didn't like his tone. He was always acting as if he was miles older than me instead of just five years. "It's just a glass of wine, Josh, not a flight of tequila shots. Not that there would be anything wrong with that."

He returned the glass to its coaster. "You're right. I'm just not much of a wine drinker. I don't suppose you have beer?"

I did from the last time he'd visited. I nodded and disappeared into the kitchen and by the time I came back with his favorite brand of beer, he was reading one of the quizzes I had been grading.

"I would have flunked your test. I don't know half of this stuff."

"That's because you were a lousy student."

He chuckled and accepted the bottle. "True, and that's why I'm here."

Tensing, I sat down on the chair next to the couch and tucked my legs off to the side so the hole near my knee wouldn't show too much.

"I'm really busy these days, Josh. I'm not sure I can help you."

I already knew what he was going to ask. He wanted help with his latest game. The last one we'd worked on together was set during the Revolutionary War. Josh was proud that his games were steeped in historically accurate details, which combined with state of the art graphics made them hot sellers.

"I really need you, Mia." He hesitated for a moment, the bottle inches from his lips. "If it's money, I can pay you."

Shit, now he wanted to offer me cash. As a lowly-paid teacher I wasn't exactly awash in greenbacks. The girls were talking about going on vacation during Spring Break — sort of a destination bachelorette party for Shelby — and I desperately wanted to go but my bank account was tragic. The expenses piling up in the next year for my sister's wedding were daunting. It wasn't cheap being maid of honor.

Honor, my ass. They ought to call it Maid of Money.

"I couldn't take your money. It wouldn't be right."

It would be helpful but not right. Josh was a family friend.

And I'm trying to not spend time with him too. I need to make sure I remember that.

Josh's gaze ran over the living room before coming back to settle on me. He'd helped me paint the walls when I'd moved in. "If I can't pay you, then maybe I can do something for you. Do you need anything done around here? Something a big strong man can help you with?"

A million filthy dirty thoughts ran through my mind. If my mother could have seen them she would have fainted dead away in horror. Shelby, on the other hand, would have hooked me up to a bunch of electrodes and studied my brain waves. Then she would have written a paper about it and presented it at some abnormal psychology convention.

"No, there's nothing you can do for me."

A slash of lightning lit up the sky outside and a loud rumble of thunder shook the windows.

Even Mother Nature knew I was lying.

CHAPTER THREE

Josh

I HADN'T ANTICIPATED Mia's hesitation to help me. She'd always seemed happy to do it in the past and really seemed to enjoy it, too. She was a terrible actress, so I doubt she'd been pretending. Maybe Luke was right and she did have a new boyfriend taking up all of her time. It might explain why she'd grown her hair out when she usually kept it shorter. She was even wearing mascara on a Saturday afternoon at home.

I took a drink of my beer and decided to go in using the money tactic. As a teacher she wasn't rolling in dough and she was always pinching pennies, especially after she'd bought the condo a few years ago. Yet she'd always insisted on paying her own way whenever we hung out together. That's how she'd started helping me in the first place. I'd wanted to pay for the whole damn pizza myself, so I'd suggested that she take a look at my World War II zombie game in return. Within an hour, she'd corrected several historical mistakes. From then on, I'd done nothing without her checking it first.

"If you're doing a job for me, Mia, then you should be compensated for it. You work as hard or harder than many people on the project, but you only get paid in pizza and chocolate."

For the first time today she smiled, showing off the cute dimples in her cheeks. "I like pizza and chocolate."

"I bet you'd like money, too." A thought occurred to him. "You might need the extra cash for Shelby's wedding present or something. Have they set a date?"

Her gaze dropped to her hands, her fingers laced together. "September. The wedding is in September."

"So it might be helpful to have another income stream." I kept the pressure up. Defeat wasn't an option here. "I bet there will be parties and things that you'll want to buy a new outfit for."

She finally looked up at him, her top teeth sunk into her full bottom lip. "You're not making this easy."

"I'm not trying to. I really need your help. I'm hopelessly stuck on this game. I haven't made any progress in weeks and even Luke is starting to get antsy."

"You've never missed a deadline."

I never had and I didn't want to start now. I had a date in my head all set for the roll out of the new game. To make it, I had to meet all the milestones along the way. This was one of the first ones.

"I'd like to keep that record going. I promise I won't take up too much of your time. Please, Mia?"

I realized I hadn't really ever asked her until then, and I sure as hell hadn't said please. Even if I paid her she was still doing me a gigantic favor.

She sighed heavily and I knew that I'd won. She was going to do it.

"Okay, but I need something from you too. I don't want

your money but if you would come speak at our career day assembly I'd be very grateful. You have a job doing something creative and that you love. I think the kids need to hear about that."

It might have helped me to hear about other careers besides accountant and cop in my teenage years. I always thought I was strange. It would have been nice to see someone who was successful doing their own thing.

"Of course, I'll do it."

My phone chimed in my pocket and I pulled it out, checking the screen. Trisha. She was persistent, I'd give her that. I'd had lunch with her today and she was already trying to plan my evening. I'd probably let her. Now that Mia had agreed to help I was much more relaxed and confident of making the finish date.

"Sorry," I apologized, typing out a quick response. "Trisha wants to know what I want for dinner."

"Oh…it's fine. Take your time."

Mia wasn't all that fond of cell phones because her students were constantly using them in class when she was trying to teach. I quickly shoved it back into my pocket.

"Send me the information and I'll be there." I stood, not wanting to take up more of her time. From what I could see she was deep into a grading session. Besides, I wanted her to finish today so she could help me tomorrow. "Can we get together tomorrow afternoon? I have Sunday lunch with Mom and Dad but after that I'm free."

She might have plans with her boyfriend, though. If she had one. She certainly was pretty enough to attract any man she wanted. Not in an obvious way, but in a really nice fresh way.

"I have lunch with my mom and dad, too," she replied, uncurling from her spot on the chair and walking with me to the door. Her sweats had a hole in the knee and I couldn't help but think how adorable she looked standing there in clothes that were clearly two sizes too big for her. "But I can meet you at your place by two. Is that okay?"

"Sounds good. Thanks again. You won't regret it."

I would make sure she wouldn't. I was planning to pay her even though she said she didn't want it. I should have done that a long time ago. Now I was feeling a little guilty. From her reaction to my request today and all of my earlier calls and texts, I clearly hadn't been appreciating her contributions enough.

I pulled my phone from my pocket and held it up. "Next time answer my texts, okay? I was beginning to get a complex with the way you were avoiding me."

"I wasn't avoiding you."

She had been, but I didn't want to argue when she'd just agreed to help me.

"I hope not. I'd hate to think that I'd lost one of my best friends."

I heard her reply just as her front door closed.

"Perish the thought, Josh."

TRISHA. JOSH'S GIRLFRIEND'S name was Trisha.

I'd met many of his girlfriends over the years, so I knew the drill. They were all extremely attractive and usually smart and successful, too. Josh didn't date airheads or bitches. I'd liked all of the ones that I'd met because they appeared to be genuinely good people. I didn't have any reason to believe that Trisha would be any different.

It would have been easier all of these years to have been secretly in love with him if the women in his life had been lacking. I could have consoled myself with the fact that Josh didn't love me because he had terrible taste in women. But he didn't.

Maybe it said something about me.

It was obvious I wasn't very smart because I'd given in to his pleas as if my backbone was made of the green Jell-O my grandmother used to bring to family gatherings. He'd barely had to make an argument and I'd easily agreed to help him. I couldn't deny that deep down I wanted to do it. We'd had so much fun in the past working on his games. There had been long days, late nights, and lots of pizza but we'd been a team and I'd liked that.

Avoiding Josh had been difficult, but refusing him when he was right in front of me was damn near impossible. It looked like I was going to be spending some quality time with the man I desperately wanted to fall out of love with.

The plan to never see him hadn't worked. I need a new and improved plan. One that was foolproof. And I needed it before tomorrow afternoon.

CHAPTER FOUR

Josh

I F I STILL lived at home I'd weigh three hundred pounds. My mom loved to cook and it was even better when the whole family was assembled in one house. We didn't do it every Sunday but we tried to get together about once a month.

It was funny how years could go by and not much had changed. Luke and I still hung out with Dad in the garage until dinner time and Mom spent most of her time in the kitchen. The only thing that was different was that Luke's wife Rachel helped her. Mom was teaching Rachel all the secret recipes that had been handed down from her mother and grandmother. Tradition was important to my parents and if I was honest, it was important to me, too. I'd really come to depend on the normalcy of these Sunday dinners when my life became too hectic and crazy.

"Did you boys make any progress on the car this morning?"

Another thing that never changed. My mom asked us that same question every Sunday, and every time my dad would reply the same way.

"We did. Should be done in a few weeks."

Now my dad has been restoring that 1966 cherry red Mustang since I was in high school. It had been a real piece of junk the day he'd pulled me into the garage and announced that if I was going to learn to drive I also needed to learn how to maintain a vehicle. My very first oil change was on that Mustang. Me, Luke, and my dad had worked on the car all through my high school years and at one point I thought he might give it to me as a graduation present. No such luck. Dad had fallen in love with the muscle car and now it was his baby. Although he could easily call it "done," he loved to hang out in the garage and tinker with it while my mom read a good book in the quiet. She once said that's what made their marriage work. They gave each other the space to do their favorite things.

I've thought about that statement a great deal over the years.

"I saw the Kelly girls next door," my father said, passing me the bowl of potatoes. It looked like Mom had put cheddar cheese in them this week. "I heard the oldest is engaged. We got an invitation to her engagement party."

Luke and I had received invitations also. The party was at a swanky hotel in the downtown area that had recently been refurbished.

"Shelby is engaged," I replied, after swallowing down a bite of roast chicken. "To some guy named Brad. Not sure of his last name."

It was on the invitation but I'd forgotten. Mia would know off the top of her head.

"Such a lovely girl," my mother said, pushing the platter of chicken closer to me and Luke. She'd made enough for an army. "And her sister too. I can't believe Mia is still single. You need to find a nice girl like her, Josh. She's such a sweet person."

My mom had never seen Mia when she was pissed. I had and it wasn't pretty. She wasn't so damn sweet then. She had that legendary redheaded temper.

"Mia's going to help Josh with his new game," Luke piped up, a shit eating grin on his face. "They're seeing each other this afternoon."

Rachel elbowed her husband and I gave him a kick under the table. Luke was bored and had decided to stir up trouble. Asshole.

"It's just business," I replied, although my mother's face had lit up at Luke's words. He shouldn't raise her hopes like that. "It's not a date."

Luke dumped more chicken on his plate. "That's true. Mia probably already has a boyfriend. She hasn't had much time for Josh lately."

My brother was about to get a fork stuck in his arm. He was at it again.

Annoyed, I scooped up a forkful of peas. "I don't think she has a boyfriend."

"A pretty girl like Mia?" my mother said with a frown. "I'm sure she does. But if she doesn't, you should ask her out."

Those peas lodged in my throat. "What? No. No, I'm not going to ask her on a date."

My mom seemed perplexed by how adamant I was. "Why not? You like her, don't you? Do you think she's attractive?"

"Of course, I like Mia." I sighed, not wanting to discuss my love life with my parents. I wasn't sixteen anymore. Hell, I hadn't discussed it even then. Our last conversation about my love life consisted of my old man pressing a pack of condoms in my hand and telling me that no meant no. "But it's not like that between us. We're friends. Besides I'm dating someone, Mom. Trisha. She's a corporate attorney."

Beautiful, smart, successful, and she wasn't looking for a serious relationship. Trisha was perfect. Mia, on the other hand, was the type of girl you married. You didn't fuck her and then forget to call the next day. You picked out china, flatware, and minivans with Mia.

"You should bring Trisha for Sunday dinner then."

There was no way I was going to do that. Inviting a woman here to meet my parents carried all sorts of serious connotations that I wasn't willing to even think about.

"Maybe I'll do that."

Luke snorted but I kicked him again under the table. It was all his fault this whole conversation had started to begin with. I didn't even know why he was acting like an ass about Mia. She was one of my best friends but that didn't mean I wanted to shag her. I didn't think about her like that.

Except now that Luke had brought it up, I couldn't help but wonder... Did she have a boyfriend? Was he even good enough for her?

I highly doubted it.

★　★　★

Mia

I SHOWED UP at Josh's front door with my shiny new *fall out of love with Josh* plan. It was so simple I don't know why I had never thought about it before. All I had to do was concentrate on all of Josh's worst qualities. All the ways he wasn't even close to perfect. Already I had a few items on the list.

He was annoying when he wanted something. I'd always called it persistence but semantics were everything. From now on I was calling it pushy and self-centered.

He was a workaholic. Once again names were important. I used to say that he was hard working and ambitious but now I was going to describe it as a dog eat dog mentality that made him selfish with his time for family and friends.

I was so happy with the first two items on my list that I hadn't properly prepared myself for all his good qualities when he opened his front door. Damn him, he looked good. Really, really good. He'd thrown on a faded pair of denims and a blue cable knit sweater as the weather had turned much colder today. It looked like we might have an early winter this year.

At least that's what my dad had said at lunch today and he was a regular reader of the *Farmer's Almanac* for the last half century or so. He also believed that wooly worms could predict the weather. All you need to do is look at the reddish-brown bands on them. Narrow meant a harsh winter and wider meant a milder one.

"You made it," Josh said, stepping back so I could cross the threshold and giving me a dazzling smile. It really should be illegal to be that handsome. "And you're only ten minutes late. I think that's a record for you."

He was always giving me crap about my punctuality. No one knew better than I did that I was late all the time. I was the one rushing around, after all.

"Bite me."

I quickly catalogued that his reminding me about being late was sort of petty. Another poor trait for my list. This was going to be so easy. I'd be out of love with him by dinnertime. I should have done this years ago.

Josh just laughed and took my coat, hanging it in the foyer closet. Another strike against him. He was fussy. I would have simply draped the darn thing over a chair.

"I hope you're ready to work. I have lots of ideas but I don't know what to do with them."

I had to admit that was a good trait. Josh always had lots of amazingly creative ideas. He was full to the brim with them and he'd once joked that he was going to have to live to be two hundred to be able to use them all.

"Let me see what you've have."

As usual, he'd placed his storyline out on the long wall of his television-slash-game room. He'd painted an entire twelve-foot wall with white board paint so he could lay out a story line easily, adding and erasing as needed. From what I could see, this one looked much more sparse than what I'd witnessed in the past.

I'd been to Josh's home about a million times so I knew it as well as my own. When he'd purchased the three bedroom, three bath ranch in a brand-new subdivision on the outskirts of town, I'd thought that perhaps he was thinking about proposing to his latest girlfriend. That idea was thrown out of the window when he'd asked me to help him pick out the furniture. No woman was going to want a sofa picked out by another female. He and I had spent several weekends strolling through furniture show-rooms and home centers selecting dining sets, throw pillows, and even art for the walls.

He liked simple, clean lines. The furniture was mission style and the decor was all done in beige and blue. The couch was overstuffed and I knew for a fact that Josh liked to nap there on Saturday afternoons.

"I'll get you a soda while you look at it," Josh said before rummaging in the refrigerator. His home had an open floor plan and the only thing that separated the kitchen from the game room was a gigantic marble island. All the appliances were stainless steel because hey, why not? "Root beer okay?"

What did this man have against caffeine? I should have brought my own legal stimulant.

"Whatever you have is fine."

He buried his head in the fridge for a moment. "I know you're cursing me right now."

Actually, I'm thrilled. Another item to add to my list. This was like shooting fish in a barrel, although I'm not sure why anyone would ever do something like that. Didn't make much sense.

"You'd be wrong. I love root beer."

He poured the foamy liquid over ice. "I have brownies with icing for dessert."

"Did you make them?"

I already knew the answer.

"I bought them, it's almost the same thing."

"It's not even close. Did you get them at the good bakery or the grocery store?"

He gave me that smile again, reaching out to brush a strand of hair off my cheek with his finger. The wind had turned my curls into a rat's nest. "The bakery, of course. I stopped after Sunday dinner. Nothing is too good for you."

He had charm in spades. For a creative geek, he was surprisingly extroverted. Okay, that was another good quality. I grudgingly added it to the pro side of the list. Wait…when had I started a pro side? Spending any time with Josh was a slippery slope. One minute I was fine and then…bam! I was sloppy in love again.

This might be harder than I thought.

CHAPTER FIVE

Mia

AFTER WE'D FIXED Josh's story draft, he'd made cheese-burgers for dinner. He was a decent chef and the entire kitchen smelled heavenly. I was starving and my stomach gurgled in anticipation as we sat down at the island to eat. Just like always, right next to each other.

While we ate, we chatted about his new game. I could tell he was excited. It was a good idea and once I'd cleaned up all his historical inaccuracies it had really come together. He'd clearly watched too many gangster movies and he didn't even know how Prohibition actually came about. Once I'd given him the background, he'd practically jumped around the room, drawing out ideas and making notes. I didn't play video games but I always made an exception for Josh's. Or at least I tried to. I sucked at games in general.

Josh pushed his plate away and patted his stomach. He'd eaten every single bite of his burger and fries. He wouldn't gain an ounce, either. That alone should make me hate his guts.

"I couldn't have done this without you, Mia. Thank you."

"I know. You're welcome."

Chuckling, he stood to clear our plates. "And you're modest, too. Seriously, Luke was tearing his hair out as the deadline approached and you weren't returning my calls. He was so rattled that he thought you might have a serious boyfriend."

I didn't like the tone in which Josh said that. As if it was so impossible that I could attract a man. I had, indeed, had men that adored me. None currently, of course, but that wasn't the point.

"But you didn't think that?"

I sounded miffed and he must have picked up on it because he was intently rinsing the dishes before placing them in the dishwasher. Normally he would have let the plates hang out in the sink.

"That wasn't my first thought but of course it was a possibility." He dropped their silverware into the plastic basket. I watched his hands, fascinated as always by his long fingers. I'd imagined too many times what those digits could do. "Do you?"

Was he interested? Was he…jealous? Doubtful, but he certainly had seemed put out that I hadn't jumped on his text messages like a dog on a bone.

"Am I what?"

I sure as hell wasn't going to make this easy for him.

He finally had to look at me since the dishes were all done. "Dating someone."

I wasn't at the moment, but he didn't need to know that. In fact, the less he knew about my personal romantic life the better. I didn't want him to know just how pathetic I had been lately.

"Are you?" I asked, jonesing for time to come up with a witty answer.

He shrugged as if it was a foregone conclusion. "Yes, her

name is Trisha."

Ah, the infamous Trisha from the text yesterday.

I hadn't really thought this through. By asking him, I'd opened myself up to having to answer his question. Shit. I need to come up with an answer lickety-split.

"I don't know if I would call it dating."

There. A vague, noncommittal answer. Maybe he'd let me leave it at that.

He frowned, wiping down the island with a dishtowel. "Then what would you call it?"

A little story. A fib. A lie, perhaps.

"I'm keeping things casual."

I sounded like a guy, which I actually kind of liked. I smiled triumphantly, daring him to ask me more personal questions about my love life. I was pretty sure Josh wouldn't want to tread anywhere near that statement.

"Casual," he repeated, nodding his head. "That's probably wise. You're still young. No sense getting tied down at your age."

Jesus, Mary, and the camel, he acted like I was a teenager. I was over thirty, and in some cultures a withered up old maid.

Thank the gods, I wasn't in any of those cultures.

He wasn't done talking, though.

"You know, just don't believe everything a guy tells you."

I'd learned that at ten when Billy Darden had one of his friends tell me he liked me but I found him kissing Marcy Edelman behind the swings at recess.

"Are you trying to say that all men are pigs?"

"All men are...focused. You just need to be careful. It's fine to date around but don't..."

Focused on getting laid. He didn't seem to be able to end his sentence so I did it for him.

"But don't sleep around?"

Rubbing the back of his neck, he looked uncomfortable. He ought to, trying to give me romance advice like he was my uncle. Or the health teacher in high school.

"Well…yeah."

"Gosh, Dad, are you saying that boys won't respect me? Or marry me? And move me into a little house with a white picket fence with two kids and a dog? Gee whiz, I guess I should give up that part time job as a pole dancer on the edge of town."

His brows shot up to his hairline and then he burst into laughter. We were both holding our sides and I had a few tears leak out of my eyes.

"A pole dancer on the edge of town?" Josh was laughing so hard he could barely get the words out. "Where did you come up with that?"

"Didn't you hear? They put a tittie bar out by the highway. Our little town is growing up." I lightly smacked his forehead with the heel of my palm. "You need to get out more."

"Tittie bar," he sighed, shaking his head. "I've always hated that word."

I wagged a finger under his nose. He could be so uptight sometimes. I put it down to growing up in a house with only a brother and no sisters. "What would you rather I call them? Boobs? Breasts? Fun bags? Tatas? Bazongas? It's a topless bar, okay? The twins are free, if you get my drift. I just want to know how a red blooded American male had no idea a nudie bar opened up within a twenty-mile radius."

I, on the other hand, had grown up with an older sister and we'd talked about everything. Most especially boobs.

"I've been busy." His eyes narrowed. "Where did you hear about it?"

Did he actually think that I'd filled out an application? My boobs were still up and firm but I wasn't the greatest dancer.

"Shelby," I answered promptly. "She wants to go out and interview all the dancers to find out if they all hate their dad."

"She thinks they hate their dad?"

"She thinks everyone hates their dad, or their mother."

He seemed to ponder my answer and then came around the island, placing both hands on the back of my barstool and turning me so that I was facing the pool table. I caught a whiff of his body wash and the room spun for a moment. He smelled so incredibly good. He always had.

Dammit, I knew what was next. That stupid table was Josh's pride and joy. Somehow I was always getting roped into a game of eight ball.

"No."

"Yes."

"No, and I mean it."

I did mean it. I was terrible at games. All of them. He just wanted to win and I was an easy target.

"Please?"

"No."

"With sugar on top?"

"No."

"With brownies and fudge icing on top?"

I could feel my will to resist weakening. He knew me far too well.

"There better be chocolate chips."

"There will be."

Another item to add to my list. He was a sneaky bastard, too. How come I wasn't out of love with him yet? This wasn't working like I'd planned.

CHAPTER SIX

Josh

ABOUT HALFWAY THROUGH dinner I'd realized just how much I'd missed Mia these last several weeks. She was always fun and easy to be around. She wasn't the demanding type always complaining about it being too hot or too cold. She did get cranky when she was hungry but it was actually kind of cute to see her grump around until she was fed.

She was also brilliant when it came to helping me with my historical story lines and this time was no exception. Within two hours she'd managed to help me whip the game into shape and I could definitely finish without issue. I'd make that deadline after all.

Mia was, however, a terrible pool player. She didn't have a competitive bone in her body either, which didn't help. If she had, she'd have been driven to get better at some point in her life, but at the rate she was going she would get her ass kicked by everyone on the planet.

"You suck at this."

She gave me a sour look as she bent over the edge of the table to make her shot. The tip of the cue stick hit at an awkward angle, sending the ball skittering across the green felt table in the opposite direction of the intended target. Mia straightened and sighed as the ball smacked into one of mine, sending it directly into the nearby pocket.

"I told you I didn't want to do this. You must really hate me."

"Frankly, I keep thinking you'll get better at it. Thanks for the help, by the way. I only have two more plus the eight ball."

"If you were my friend you'd throw the game."

I probably should be merciful but my innate competitive streak wouldn't allow me to do that. Something inside of me always drove me to win. At a moment like this, I was ashamed of it. Mia was a sweet girl and every instinct was telling me to crush her like a bug.

What is wrong with me?

"How about I be a better friend and help you? If you were just a little better you wouldn't need me to throw the game for you."

A bit of an exaggeration. Mia was going to have to get a whole lot better to beat me but she would at least be competitive.

"Just how are you going to help me? You're the one that taught me the game in the first place."

I bent over and quickly made my shot, a hell of a lot more sloppy than I usually would. Now it was Mia's turn again. I'd set up a nice corner shot for her. She could do this.

"Okay," I said, going over to where she was standing and leading her to the right side of the table. "Stand right here."

"I'm a lost cause. Leave me to my misery."

"No way. This is an easy shot. You can make it."

"I hate you for this, Josh Henry."

"You're going to love me in a minute."

I placed my hands on her shoulders and gently pushed her forward so we were both bent at the waist, her body tucked into mine. I placed my hands over hers and moved them into the correct position. Her skin was soft underneath my own, smooth to the touch. The smell of vanilla and coconut wafted around my head and a few stray auburn curls tickled my nose. Mia smelled...amazing. Her shampoo had mixed with her own natural scent and it was warm and intoxicating. Before I could stop myself I filled my lungs with it again, taking a deep breath and closing my eyes to savor it.

Her pert little behind was pressed against my groin and that was when all the trouble began. Between her alluring scent and her well-shaped ass my cock had a mind of its own. It was quickly draining the blood from my brain and affecting my ability to make even halfway decent decisions. If I didn't put some distance between Mia and I immediately I was going to do something really stupid, like kiss the silky soft skin on her neck which was only inches from my lips.

For the first time since I'd known Mia I was suddenly wondering how her skin felt all over. Was she paler on her breasts and belly? Did she have those delicious freckles everywhere?

I had a vision of my tongue tracing those freckles on her creamy flesh.

Bad. So very bad. This was all Luke's fault, mentioning how hot she'd become. I needed to punch him in the nose on Monday morning.

I stepped away as if I'd been scalded and before Mia became aware of my predicament. The last thing we needed between us was my hard dick. It was a good way to ruin a friendship.

I loosened my hold on her and moved away, taking a deep breath of relief. I should never have been that close to begin with and I wouldn't make that mistake again.

"So…just try and make the shot."

The words came out slightly strangled but Mia didn't seem to notice, so intent on sinking the ball. The tip of the cue struck solidly and the ball glided across the surface of the pool table before falling into the pocket. She'd done it.

Mia did a fist pump in the air. "Yes! I did it."

Letting out a squeal of joy she dropped the cue on the table and threw her arms around my neck, all the while hopping up and down. Her body rubbed against mine and I was once again highly aware that Mia had some sweet curves. My cock still hadn't retreated from earlier and was now standing at full attention, ready for action, except that there wasn't going to be any. This was Mia, my little neighbor. I'd helped her learn how to ride a bike, for Christ's sake. I wasn't going to teach her to ride me, too.

This all had to stop. I quickly stepped back and pasted a smile on my face while turning so that my lower half wasn't pressed against her.

"You did great. That was awesome. See? You can do this. With a little practice, you'll be beating me and everyone else."

She was still hopping up and down excitedly, her green eyes sparkling and her cheeks a rosy pink. She looked adorable.

"I really did it," she crowed, clasping her hands together. "Thank you, Josh. You are a good teacher."

I'm a total lecher, in actuality.

"You did it. I just helped a little." I cast a desperate glance over my shoulder. "How about we have some of those brownies now? I could use some dessert."

I could use a double whiskey but I'd wait until Mia went home.

She licked her full lips in anticipation and I almost groaned out loud. Shit. This was only getting worse. How do I politely ask her to leave? She could take the brownies to go.

"I'm hungry, too. I'll get the plates and forks."

Good idea. I'll just be over here looking for my sanity. Clearly I've lost it if my reaction to Mia tonight is any indication. She's my friend and I don't want to ruin that.

I don't have sexual feelings for her.

The best thing about Mia Kelly was that she wasn't my girlfriend.

CHAPTER SEVEN

Mia

TRUE TO HIS word, Josh showed up the next week at my school ready to talk to the students about his work and business. I should have known his mere presence would cause a ruckus among the teenagers – and he did – but what I hadn't bargained on was grown women acting like simpering fools around him. Did they have no shame? At least I had my dignity.

My fellow female teachers were swooning as if Josh was some sort of movie star. He was good looking but not *that* good looking.

Tina, the honors math teacher, tugged at my arm as Josh stood in front of the crowded auditorium taking questions about his work. "Are you two dating?"

I didn't turn around. Instead I kept my gaze trained on Josh who was charming a senior cheerleader who had asked about art school. Well...he'd had plenty of experience. He'd dated the captain of the cheerleaders several times.

"No, he's just a friend of many years."

Tina snorted and then giggled. "If he was my friend I'd make him a friend with benefits double quick. He's a hunk and a half."

"He's not really my type."

"Which part don't you like? Tall, dark, and handsome? The smile? The wide shoulders? Oh, it must be the flat abs? That's probably it. Honey, he's everyone's type."

This time I did turn to address her. "You're a married woman."

"Married but not dead. I think we need to check your pulse, though."

If they did they'd find it racing far too fast. Just being in the same room with Josh was enough to get my heart going. When he'd showed up, he'd looked amazing, actually sporting a tie to go with his button-down shirt. He'd tamed his curls slightly with some gel and his square jaw was shaved so smoothly I wanted to reach out and run my fingers over it.

"I'm fine. Like I said, he's a friend. Once you get to know him he's just any other guy."

Sure. Right. I was the freakin' Rock of Gibraltar.

I stood in the wings of the stage watching Josh talk about his video game business. He was smiling and animated, totally excited about sharing his career with these kids. It was clear he loved what he did and that just made him all the more attractive.

The jerk.

When his presentation – slash – question period was over he ducked offstage with me, grinning like a loon. Tina had gone back on stage to announce the next guest for career day, her family physician.

"So? How'd I do? Was it okay?"

The one attribute Josh had plenty of was confidence, so I assumed he was playing at not being sure how it went. He had to know from the thunderous applause he'd received that he'd hit it out of the park.

"You did great," I assured him. "They were really interested in what you had to say. You made it entertaining for them."

A feat that wasn't easy with teenagers. They had cell phones and YouTube. And the opposite sex.

"It was more fun than I thought it would be. They're very inquisitive."

I led us out of the auditorium area and down the hallway toward my classroom where he'd left his jacket. "Don't believe everything you read about how awful teenagers are these days. They're a lot like we were at that age. Some are ambitious and driven, some are quiet and shy, some are loud and want attention, and some are just trying to make it through high school. Most of my students are intelligent and well behaved, even if they aren't interested in the subject. I don't find that their attention spans are any shorter or that they're socially stunted from being online. I don't think we need to worry about the next generation at all."

We walked into my empty classroom. All of the juniors and seniors were at the assembly.

"I'll sleep better at night knowing that." He shrugged into his blue pea coat. "You handle them beautifully, by the way, and I can tell they all like you. I think a few of the boys have a crush on you. They were looking a little starry eyed when you were directing them to their seats."

There had been one young man last year who had become something of a nuisance but other than that I hadn't had any issues.

"I'm sure that's not the case."

Chuckling, he reached into his pocket to check his phone. "I'm sure it is. If I had had a teacher as pretty as you in high school, I would have been sitting in the first row every single day even if I had pneumonia."

He thought I was that attractive? That was news. I steeled myself to show no reaction.

"Now you're just being silly."

"When I'm being silly, you'll know it. I'll stand on my head or wear a clown's costume."

I shuddered at the mere thought. "There's nothing scarier than a clown. You know they creep me out."

"You wouldn't be scared of me."

"If you were in a clown's costume I would be."

We seemed to run out of things to say and that was unusual for us. Most of the time we were talking over each other trying to say every little idea that had popped into our heads before it was gone again.

Our gazes met and for a moment I allowed myself to drown in his azure blue eyes flecked in gray right around the irises. Josh's eyes could go from icy gray when he was angry or upset to dark blue when he was happy or excited. For just a few seconds I let myself enjoy his scent and warmth, his body just inches from my own. If I wasn't in the friend zone, I would have pressed my body against his and kissed him.

This is such a terrible idea. Stop it.

I stepped back and dragged my gaze away from his, gulping in air to my starved lungs. Apparently while I'd been looking dreamily into his eyes I'd forgotten to breathe. That's how stupid this man made me. I'd forget to do something I wasn't even supposed to need to remember.

"So thanks for coming in today. The kids really enjoyed it."

"I was happy to do it."

He wasn't moving toward the door. Shouldn't he be doing that? Maybe he didn't want to go.

"Don't act too happy about it or I'll put you on the roster every single year."

"Seriously, I had fun. Your students are awesome."

"They really are."

Finally he glanced toward my classroom door. "Listen, I've worked up a storyboard I'd like you to see. Do you think you'd be free one night this week?"

Of course. Work. That's what he'd been lingering about. The game. It wasn't because he wanted to continue looking into my eyes too. For a moment I'd allowed myself to think that perhaps…

"I'll have to check my schedule. I'll text you."

I'd been right to try to avoid him. Being this close was becoming exquisite torture.

But avoiding him had been painful as well. Was this my fate? To love someone who would never love me back? That sucked and I was getting tired of it. I didn't want to be this pathetic person. But I didn't know how to make it stop. Something had to change and soon.

CHAPTER EIGHT

Josh

ANOTHER SATURDAY NIGHT date with Trisha. She was talking about a meeting she'd been in yesterday but my mind was a million miles away. Mia was avoiding my calls again. She'd said she'd text me about seeing the storyboards but she hadn't. I had texted her again. And again. This was becoming a pattern.

Trisha ate the last bite of our shared tiramisu dessert and then sat back and patted her stomach.

"That was delicious. I shouldn't have eaten it though."

If I lived to be a hundred and ten I'd never understand why women said things like this. She'd clearly wanted dessert as she'd been eyeing all the diners around us eating theirs. But she'd made me talk her into it which was stupid because I didn't care if we had dessert or not, but somehow I was put in the role of *diet spoiler.* Then she ate three-quarters of it. Every guy knows that the woman always, always, always gets the last bite of dessert.

Women. A mystery wrapped in a riddle, and tonight covered in a tight black sweater that showed off her assets nicely. Trisha had a great rack, although I was a leg man. For a moment, an unbidden image of Mia's legs drifted in front of my eyes. She'd looked spectacular in that fitted black skirt that showed off well-toned calves and a heart-shaped ass. Paired with a button down white blouse and her tortoise shell glasses balanced on her pert nose, she was every man's naughty librarian fantasy.

Don't go there. She's your friend, you horn dog.

These thoughts about Mia were beginning to become a problem. I'd barely paid any attention to Trisha tonight and I blamed my childhood friend for that.

"It was good." I caught the waiter's eye for the bill. If we got out of here soon enough I could still catch most of the football game on television. "I'll get the check and then we can go."

"What are you doing at Thanksgiving?"

If last year was anything to go by, I would be eating far too much of my mother's cooking and watching football with my brother and dad.

"Same as last year. Why?"

I asked the question casually but Trisha had my senses tingling. I'd been dating long enough to know that this wasn't an off-the-cuff question. She was going somewhere with this. I could tell by the way she'd leaned forward, placing her elbows on the table, her cheeks flushed with excitement.

"Just imagine it. Sun and sand. Tropical drinks. You and me walking along a warm beach." When I didn't answer right away, she smiled widely and clapped her hands together. "We should get away from the rat race. Go on vacation and have some fun. What do you think?"

I was thinking that the collar on my shirt was becoming far too tight. Like a noose. Trisha had told me when we started dating that she wasn't interested in anything serious. She was just out of a bad relationship and looking to have a good time.

"It sounds…"

Intimate. Like a couple. The serious kind.

Her smile fell and she sat back in her chair, a defeated look on her face. "You don't like the idea. We could go skiing instead, if you don't like the warm weather."

I loved the beach. That wasn't the issue.

"Do we have to make the decision tonight? I'd need to talk to Luke about the timing. It's a couple of months away."

I wasn't even sure I would be dating Trisha in November. I liked her and all but I already knew she wasn't *the one.*

"Sure," she replied, her voice low. "But we don't want to wait too long. Places book up fast around the holidays."

I'd hurt her feelings and I didn't mean to. We'd met at a Fourth of July party thrown by a mutual friend and I'd called her the next day. We'd had a great deal of fun and she was a wonderful woman. But the thought of being with her – and only with her – for days on end in an airplane, in a hotel, during meals and bedtime was a little much for me. Way too much togetherness. I was the kind of guy who liked seeing a female a few times a week. That was the perfect compromise of *my* time and *our* time. If we went on vacation all of *my* time would become *her* time.

I could tell I wasn't out of the woods though by the way she fiddled with her fork and studied it as if it was suddenly the most fascinating item in the room. Warning bells rang in my ears but there was no place to hide. I had to sit there and see it through.

"Josh, where would you say this relationship was going?"

Fuck. Nothing good had ever come from that question.

★ ★ ★

Mia

I PULLED INTO the parking lot of the convenience store that was located just a few blocks away from my condo. I was tired after a long day of having fun with my friends, running around like we were teenagers again. The four of us had gone to the mall to find Emmy some new clothes for work. Then later we ate dinner and saw a movie. All I wanted to do was crawl into bed and watch television but that wasn't going to happen. I had a stack of essays to grade this weekend and I needed to get a start on them. I wanted to get them back to the students by Wednesday at the latest.

Staying up late meant caffeine and lots of it, which was why I'd stopped at the EZ Mart to pick up a six pack of soda. I didn't normally keep it in the house since I was trying to cut down. There weren't any cars in the parking lot but the place was lit up brightly as usual. I stopped there quite a bit to get gas, pick up milk, and stock up on junk food. The usual late night clerk was at the register and I gave him a cheery wave as I walked in. I didn't remember his name but he was always polite and helpful.

I walked to the back of the store and grabbed a six pack of Vanilla Coke and a giant bag of M&M's. I shouldn't be eating them but in a few hours I was going to want a snack to go along with my caffeine. I headed directly to the cash register while fumbling in my purse for some cash. Triumphantly, I pulled out a twenty just as the door to the store swung open and a man dressed all in black and wearing a ski mask walked in.

My heart stuttered in my chest and my fingers tightened on the bill in my hand, crumpling it into a sweaty ball. It wasn't cold enough outside for a ski mask. Something very, very bad was about to happen and I was frozen in place. I couldn't move my legs to run away, not that fleeing was a good idea. The fact was I didn't know what to do and neither did the poor clerk who immediately raised his hands in the air when the masked man brandished a gun.

A gun.

"Everybody just shut up and no one gets hurt." The thief pointed to the register with the barrel of his gun. "Clear it out and put it in a bag. Slowly. Don't be a hero and you get to go home to your family tonight."

There were three of us – myself, the clerk, and another man wearing dark sunglasses at night, who actually looked a trifle bored by the whole thing. Like it was just another day. It took me a minute to realize he was with the thief and he also had a gun, although he wasn't waving it around. But it was at that moment that he seemed to notice me.

"You," he said, pointing the gun at my chest. I'd never had a gun pointed directly at me and you'd be surprised by how scary it was. I was no superhero and if he wanted my purse he could have it with my compliments. It wasn't even a real Prada, just a knockoff I'd purchased at a flea market. I just wanted to live through this. "Don't make a move and keep those hands where I can see them."

I hadn't planned on it and couldn't even if I wanted to. Sweat had pooled on the back of my neck and under my arms, giving me what I assumed was a stink of desperation and terror.

Shelby had explained it to me once but I had barely listened. Next time I would listen. I would for sure.

I hope there's a next time.

The man pointing a gun at me didn't have all of his face covered like the other guy and I couldn't help but think that I might be able to pick him out of a lineup. Which was bad. So incredibly bad. He might not want to leave any witnesses. What if he was just leading us on by saying we'd be okay and then when they got their money he'd shoot us dead without a second thought?

I didn't want to be dead. I desperately needed to live and do all of the things that I'd always said that I wanted to do but never seemed to get around to actually doing. I hadn't had the great love of my life yet, unless you counted Josh.

I definitely couldn't count him.

I hadn't gotten married or had a baby or climbed a mountain or visited Paris. I'd always wanted to go to the top of the Eiffel Tower but now because of this asshole I wasn't going to get a chance to do that. I was going to die young and become a cautionary tale to others about visiting convenience stores after dark. I could hear my sister telling a work colleague...

If only Mia wasn't addicted to chocolate and caffeine. She'd be alive today.

The clerk whose nametag said Randy – if I lived I would remember his name for the rest of my life – filled a brown paper bag with the money from the cash register. In the meantime, I wasn't sure how I was still standing upright because my heart was beating so fast and loud I was sure they could hear it a mile away. I was still frozen with shock and fear but those emotions were quickly turning to anger. I didn't want to be a casualty of this night. I wanted to live.

I realized at that moment that I had never really gone after what I wanted. Sure, I'd played at it but always sort of half-hearted so if I didn't get it then I could just say it was no big deal. I didn't want it bad enough to really put it all on the line and go for it. Taking chances wasn't my style. I was all about keeping to my comfort zone. It hadn't been a terrible way to live but it was no way to go forward. If I died now I wouldn't have much to show for my life. I didn't even know what they'd put on my tombstone or in my obituary.

Mia Kelly died like she lived. Standing still.

I closed my eyes for a moment and sent up a thought into the universe. I wasn't a particularly religious person but I was spiritual. If there was anyone listening perhaps they could give me a hand in my time of need.

If I survive this, I promise to go out of my comfort zone. I promise to go after what I want. No more half-assing my life. As of now, I'm a changed woman.

Randy handed the stuffed brown bag to the masked man and the two robbers began to back toward the door they'd come in. The man in shades lifted his gun and pointed it directly to my chest and bared his teeth as if he were an animal.

"Don't move a muscle until we're gone. Do you understand?"

I did understand and somehow I even managed to nod, although I think it was a reflex and not any functioning part of my brain initiating the action. The two men fled out of the entrance and into a waiting car I hadn't noticed until that moment. Their tires squealed loudly as they drove out of the parking lot. Randy rolled his eyes and reached for his phone on the back counter.

"Shit, I hate it when this happens. My boss is going to be pissed."

I placed my sweaty palms on my thighs to dry them, forgetting that I held a twenty in my hand. It fluttered to the floor but I didn't lean down to pick it up. Instead my knees gave way and I slid down to the tile, my back up against the counter. I was shaking so hard I had to hold onto my fake Prada purse with both hands. The room spun but then righted as I concentrated on my breathing. In and out. In and out. The yoga classes that Emmy and Ashlyn dragged me to were finally coming in handy.

"Hey, lady? You're not going to pass out, are you? I called the cops and they'll be here in a minute. I can call an ambulance, too. Do you want me to call an ambulance?"

Randy's voice sounded like I had my head in the sink.

"I'm not going to pass out."

But I might throw up.

I could hear the sirens in the distance. Help was almost here but I was already safe. In fact, I had been safe for far too long. I'd been sliding through life simply skimming the surface but never going too deep. That changed tonight. I'd made a deal with the universe. They'd done their part, now I had to do mine.

"I'm going to go after what I want."

If Randy thought my statement was a little strange he didn't say so. Two police cruisers pulled into the parking lot, sirens blaring and lights flashing. I'd be here for awhile giving a statement but tomorrow would be a new day.

In the morning, I'd start going after all the things I wanted in my life. First on the list?

Josh Henry.

CHAPTER NINE

Josh

I ENDED UP at Luke's house after I dropped Trisha off at her place. As I expected, he had the game on and was watching with his wife Rachel. She told me to help myself to a beer in the refrigerator, so I snagged one and joined them in the living room. We watched the game and didn't say much until halftime.

"Clearly your date didn't go well," Luke observed, digging into the chips and French onion dip on the coffee table.

"What makes you say that?"

"You were at our front door by nine-fifteen," Rachel said, returning from the kitchen with three fresh beers. "That's not a good sign."

"Maybe I wanted to talk to Luke about the new game on the drawing board."

"We should talk about that," Luke replied, sliding an arm around Rachel as she snuggled close. "On Monday morning."

"Since when do you not like to work on the weekends? You're worse than me."

Rachel's brow quirked and she shook her head. "No one is worse than you."

Okay, that might be true. But I loved what I did and I was

damn lucky to be doing it.

"So that brings us back to my original observation," Luke said. "Your date didn't go well tonight. Did you piss Trisha off?"

"You could say that," I said dryly, remembering the incredibly awkward conversation we'd had at the end of our meal. "We broke up."

To my chagrin, neither of them looked even remotely surprised.

"What was the reason this time?" Rachel asked, taking a drink from her beer bottle. "She wanted you to meet her parents? She had bad breath? She liked to watch 'Gilmore Girls'?"

It appeared that Rachel had paid more attention in those past conversations about my girlfriends than I'd given her credit for. She made me sound petty though and I didn't consider myself that way.

I wasn't…was I?

"She was pressuring me to go on vacation with her over Thanksgiving. That's almost two months away. It's only the end of September."

Rachel's eyes went wide and her mouth dropped open in mock horror. "A whole two months? That's practically a lifetime. Who does she think she is trying to make plans with you so far in advance?"

Luke was laughing but I didn't appreciate the joke at my expense.

"Ha ha, I get it. So funny. Seriously, we've only been dating since July. That's not very long."

"It's long enough when you're with the right person," Luke argued. "A week is long enough when you've met the one."

"I've never even been in the same zip code as *the one*. In fact, I'm beginning to think all of this talk about the one is a bunch of bullshit."

Rachel shot me the evil eye. "Here I am just sitting here like I'm invisible to you. Asshole."

Luckily, she and I had a really good relationship. She was the best thing that had ever happened to Luke. She knew it, too. She never gave him – or me – a hard time when we would work all weekend at his place. She simply took the opportunity to go do her own thing. I really liked that she was independent like that. They didn't live in each other's pockets. Like my parents.

"Okay, you two are each other's one but I've never met anyone like that."

"Do you want to?" Rachel challenged. "Because you've never acted like it was important to you."

"I do. Eventually."

I'd just never been in any hurry. There was plenty of time for…that.

"What does the right woman look like, Josh? What is she like?"

I had no idea really. I liked all kinds of women.

"I don't know. Pretty. Funny. Intelligent. Kind. Likes the outdoors and sports. Gets along with my family and friends. Has interests of her own. Successful in her field, but she doesn't have to make a lot of money or anything. She should just be good at what she does. Athletic would be nice. A dog lover but not cats. She should like to travel to places off the beaten path, maybe even camping or hiking Europe."

Did that sound stupid?

"She sounds like a real paragon of virtue." Luke joked. "If a woman was that perfect, she wouldn't give your ugly ass the time of day."

I flipped him the bird. "Got it. I'm no prize."

Rachel elbowed her husband before turning her attention back to me. "I'm going to tell you something that may shock you, Josh, but you need to know it. You're not special. You're pretty much like every guy I've ever dated. Scared of commitment and looking for a human being that doesn't exist. Let me ask you a question. Have you ever been dumped? Ever?"

I opened my mouth to say that of course I'd been dumped. Everyone had at one point but then I hesitated for a moment. My mind whirled with all the girls that I'd dated through the years and how each relationship had ended.

"My first girlfriend," I replied triumphantly. "Katie Torrino. She dumped me for the quarterback of the football team."

My parents wouldn't let me play football. Or rather my mom wouldn't. I'd begged and begged but she'd stood firm and dad wouldn't overrule her. If he had I probably would have lost my virginity much earlier in high school.

"But no one after that?" Rachel asked, reaching for a chip. "Why do you think that is?"

"I don't know. Is it important?"

She rolled her eyes and popped the chip into her mouth. "You don't think it's weird that you absolutely have to be the first to end things? That doesn't give you pause for even a second?"

"Maybe I just know what I want and I'm decisive. I don't want to waste time in relationships that aren't going to work

66

out."

"How would you know?" Rachel shot back. "You don't stick around long enough to find out."

"That's not fair. I stick around."

Rachel nodded and reached for another chip. The game was starting again. "Okay. I'm probably wrong."

That was it? She wasn't going to argue with me? I looked at Luke for help but he was simply smiling at his wife as if she'd done something extremely clever.

"You're just giving up?"

"Is it an argument? I made an observation and you told me that I'm wrong. End of discussion. If you don't think I'm right, then I must not be. It's fine. It's your life, after all. It doesn't affect me except when you have a bad date and end up here drinking our beer and sleeping on our couch so you don't have to drive home."

She made me sound kind of pathetic, which I certainly wasn't. I was a highly successful entrepreneur who was popular with the opposite sex. The only reason I sat home on a Friday or Saturday night was because I wanted to. Not because I had to.

"Well…good. I didn't want to argue with you."

"Same here."

"Being single doesn't bother me at all." For some reason, words were coming out of my mouth and I couldn't seem to stop them. "In fact, I was thinking about not dating for a little while. Just enjoying being single for a few months. Hang out with my friends."

Like Mia, for example.

Stop thinking about Mia.

Luke's gaze had returned to the television. The teams were back on the field for the second half.

"Sounds like a good idea."

Pushing Mia out of my brain, the idea was beginning to grow on me. Not having to worry about anyone else sounded like heaven. I was always making compromises when dating about restaurants and movies and television shows. It would be good to just be alone for awhile. Do whatever I wanted to do.

"So that's what I'm going to do. I'm going to take a break from women for a month."

I'd been dating since I was fifteen. A break sounded like just what I needed. The women would still be there in thirty days. I was single and definitely not on the prowl.

One month of just me. It was going to be great.

CHAPTER TEN

Mia

THERE HADN'T BEEN this much activity in my condo since Ashlyn's thirtieth birthday party. An epic evening that few of us could remember in its entirety. We only knew that the next morning we all felt like we had been hit by a truck.

Emmy, Ashlyn, and of course Shelby were pacing back and forth in my living room going on and on about how I could have been killed.

As if I didn't know that. My blood pressure had to still be sky high from the evening's events.

I pressed against my pounding temples with my fingertips. "Could you please sit down? I've got a horrible headache and all of you bouncing off of the walls isn't helping me."

All three of them froze but Emmy, bless her, immediately strode toward my kitchen. "I'll get you some ibuprofen. Is it still in the drawer?"

"Yes," I called to her retreating figure. "Bring two. And a whiskey. It's in the cabinet over the sink."

Shelby shook her head. "You can't drink alcohol and take pain medication. It's not good for your liver function."

My sister could not be serious. This wasn't just any old run of the mill kind of Saturday night.

"Are you saying that I have to choose between alcohol and a couple of ibuprofen?"

"Yes. I don't want to have to take you to the emergency room tonight."

Emmy returned, juggling a water bottle, a highball glass of whiskey, and two tablets. I pointed to Shelby as Emmy dumped the items on the coffee table in front of me.

"Miss I'm-not-that-kind-of-doctor says I have to choose between booze and pills. I choose booze."

I reached for the glass but of course my interfering sister couldn't let me have a breakdown in peace. She was still being pissy because I wouldn't let her call Mom and Dad until the morning. I couldn't take my mother tonight. I loved her but she would simply be far more than I could handle in my current state.

"Don't," she scolded, giving my hand a light slap. After the night I'd had she was lucky she didn't get a smack in return. A heck of a lot harder. "Alcohol is not the answer."

"What is the answer, Dr. Kelly? Therapy? Would you use Freud or Jung?"

Her expression softened and she sat down next to me on the couch, wrapping an arm around my shoulders. Usually I liked hugs and physical expressions of affection but for some reason I couldn't tolerate it tonight. I scooted away, not wanting anyone near me. This was the reason I didn't want my parents here right now.

"You do need to talk to someone about this," Shelby said softly. "If not me, then another licensed professional. You could have post-traumatic stress from this. You've been through a terrible ordeal tonight."

My sister had a firm grasp of the obvious.

"I know," I said loudly, hopping up from the couch. I felt like I was going to jump out of my skin. Every sense seemed sharpened. The colors were brighter, the smells more acute. I could feel the fabric of the couch under my fingertips. If an ant walked across the table I bet I would have been able to feel it. "I was the one there, remember? I was the one that had that gun pointed at my chest. And I said that if I survived—"

I broke off, suddenly realizing that there were three pairs of eyes staring at me, listening to every word I said.

"You made a deal?" Ashlyn asked. "What kind of deal?"

They were going to find out anyway because I was a different person now. I'd changed during those tense minutes in the convenience store. I was kind of surprised they couldn't see it. I felt like I'd just been given a second chance.

"I said that if I survived I was going to go after what I want. No more sitting back and waiting for things to come to me, happen to me. I realized tonight that I've just been phoning it in when it comes to life. Just going with it but always too afraid to go after what I want."

Emmy nodded as if she understood. "Because if you actually try but then fail you have to acknowledge that. If you don't try, then it's not on you."

"Exactly. But no more. As of tonight, I am a new person." I held out my arms dramatically. "Behold the new Mia Kelly. The new and improved version."

They didn't look as impressed as I'd hoped.

★ ★ ★

Mia

MY FRIENDS' EXPRESSIONS could only be described as dubious.

"I think you were pretty good before," Shelby said sourly. "Maybe you should pace yourself, sis. A lot of people make bargains at moments like that. You're not bound by it. Nothing bad will happen if you don't become an entirely new person. It's okay. What you did was normal."

They all thought that tonight was just a blip on the screen, an anomaly. But I knew better. I was changed and I couldn't go back to the way I was. I didn't want to.

"I don't want to live my life afraid of going after what I want anymore. I was half-asleep but now I'm awake. Wide awake. Life is short and I don't want to get to the end of it not having lived to the fullest."

Emmy rubbed at her forehead. "You're not going to climb Mount Everest or anything, are you? Because people die up there and they leave their bodies."

I shook my head, shuddering at the thought of it. "I hate the cold and you know that. There wasn't an adrenaline junkie hidden inside of me waiting to come out. I just need to start going for the things that I want. Taking a few chances here and there."

"What kind of chances are we talking about here?" Ashlyn asked. "Joining CrossFit? Becoming an amateur sleuth like in 'Murder, She Wrote'? I never understood how Jessica Fletcher dealt with all the death that followed her. You'd think she'd need therapy or something."

It was the moment to reveal my plan. Or my idea, really. I didn't quite have a plan but I was going to get one with Shelby's help.

I spread my arms out dramatically again, hoping that the second time would be the charm.

"I'm going after Josh Henry."

There was silence and then they all began talking at once, each one louder than the last to be heard. Having just come through a traumatic event, the noise was too much for my poor assaulted senses. I covered my ears and closed my eyes.

"Can you keep it down?" I yelled. "I can't even hear myself think."

They all fell silent and by some telepathic agreement they let Shelby speak first.

"You're going after Josh? I can't say that I'm shocked."

Ashlyn nodded. "I think this is a positive development. Go after him and see what happens. Then you'll know for sure either way."

"Exactly," Emmy said. "If it doesn't work out then you'll know and you can move on with your life."

With friends like these who needed enemies?

"Your belief in me is so heartwarming," I said, my tone dripping with sarcasm. "You're already preparing me for failure. I don't think it's a surprise why I've lived scared all these years. No one believes in me. I want you to know it's hurtful."

These traitors were my best friends in the world. What did other people think of me?

"I believe in you," my sister said softly. "But if Josh were interested…"

Her voice trailed away and I had to acknowledge the truth of her statement. If he was interested he would have done something about it by now. He wasn't faint-hearted when it came to the ladies.

"I know what you're saying but I think that's just because he doesn't see me as dating material. He sees me as the neighbor kid. I have to change that and you're going to help me, Shelby. Do you still have your book? I'm going to need it."

I'd said the magic words. The book. Her eyes lit up and she dug into that oversized monstrosity of a bag that had cost her a small fortune. But then she might have the right idea.

Note to self. Replace fake Prada bag. Better a genuine Target than a fake designer.

"I do have it. Are you really going to use it? This is so exciting."

Even Ashlyn and Emmy had perked up. They might not believe in me but they believed in Shelby's stupid book.

Or maybe they were just looking forward to me making a fool of myself with Josh. It was certainly one possible outcome.

Shelby held up the book triumphantly. "I can't believe we're doing this. My little sister is going to set a man trap."

Josh Henry, get ready because here I come.

CHAPTER ELEVEN

Josh

THE MONTH OF me started the next morning. As I sat in the living room and drank my coffee, I sent another text to Mia. I really did want her to see the new storyboards. I valued her opinion but she was starting to piss me off when she didn't answer. Maybe she really did have a guy that was keeping her busy. Looking back at our conversation, she hadn't really answered my question directly.

I didn't have Sunday dinner with my folks today so I could happily sit around the house in my boxers, eat pizza, and watch football, although it sounded incredibly lazy and indulgent. I normally didn't like not being busy doing something. I could hit the gym or perhaps go for a run, maybe do some grocery shopping. I could even cook an actual meal. I'd been eating way too much takeout and living on way too little sleep. A nap wouldn't be out of the question either.

It's all about me today. What I want to do.

I checked my phone again and frowned when I saw that Mia hadn't returned my text. Honestly, if she couldn't be bothered then I should just let it go. I headed into the bedroom to change into workout clothes. A run was exactly what I needed to clear my head for the rest of the day. The weather was actually sunny and mild, around sixty-five degrees. Not bad. I should enjoy the good weather while it lasted.

My run turned into a trip to the park's obstacle course and then on to Chance's Pub for lunch – a meatball grinder dripping with mozzarella. I sat around and shot the shit with Chance for awhile as we watched football on one of the big screens. By the time I returned back to the house I was in a pretty decent mood. I'd hardly thought about Mia at all.

My phone started beeping as I was untying my shoelaces. I hopped over to it on one foot, hoping it was Mia. No such luck. It was Luke and he probably wanted me to meet him at the office. I would do it too, but after my shower.

"Hey, Luke. What's going on?"

"I just talked to Mom. Have you heard the news?"

Sitting down on the edge of the bed, I finished untying my laces. "News? No, Mom hasn't called me. Is everything okay?"

I didn't like the tone in Luke's voice. He'd sounded slightly panicked. Not enough that I thought anything was wrong with our parents but enough that something wasn't right.

"Mom talked to Mia and Shelby's parents today. I guess Mia was caught in some sort of convenience store robbery last night. She was being held hostage or something. Had a gun pointed at her chest and everything. She's okay but shook up. Her parents were cooking up a storm from what Mom said so they can take Sunday dinner to her place. You might want to give Mia a call and see if she's alright."

Holy shit, I'd been texting Mia about my petty work issues and she'd been on the wrong end of a gun? Fuck. I wanted to reel back all of my messages to her but I couldn't do that. I could only apologize. She'd had a good reason not to return my calls last night and today. I was a stupid bastard.

"But she's okay?" I pressed, still not sure that one of my best childhood friends was healthy and alive. "Did they take her to the hospital or anything?"

"I don't think so. She wasn't hurt or shot. Just scared, which is totally understandable."

I'd seen Mia scared once or twice. She didn't like heights. Or clowns. Or snakes. Or spiders. But a gun was a whole different thing. No one expects that. Nothing could prepare her.

"I'll call her," I said when I realized that Luke was waiting for me to say something. "I'm glad you let me know. Jesus, that's awful."

"It is. She could have died."

That statement hit me right in the gut, taking my breath away.

I didn't want to lose my friend.

★ ★ ★

SHELBY SPENT THE night at my place while Emmy and Ashlyn went home. They were back early in the morning however, cooking breakfast and chatting about random topics. Mom and Dad called and said they were bringing over lunch. They were a little upset with me because I didn't call them last night, although they were more angry with Shelby. I just couldn't take all of their fussing and hovering. I could barely handle having my friends around me. I was much better this morning however as I inhaled the delicious aroma of bacon. Emmy was asking me about my students this year and the other teachers. It was a ruse to keep me from thinking about last night.

They needn't have bothered because I wasn't pondering the robbery too much, anyway. What I was thinking about was my newfound zest for life in general, and going for Josh in particular. Ashlyn had made chocolate chip pancakes to go with the bacon and we sat around my living room, plates balanced on our knees. My kitchen table was covered with history essays and in no shape to entertain guests.

I'd sat at the far end of the couch next to the side table where I'd placed Shelby's book. Paging through it, I had to admit I was impressed. My big sister had written a book. She'd done it. It was a big damn deal. People were always saying they were going to write a book but few ever did. It was a real accomplishment and she should be proud of herself. I was proud of her.

"Are you ready for love?" I read out loud the title of the first chapter. "I think the answer to that question is a resounding yes. On to Chapter Two."

"Wait," Shelby cautioned, holding her fork up. "Don't jump around. This is a system. You need to find out if you're really ready for true love. If you can't love and accept yourself, no one else will either."

I placed a hand over my heart. "I truly and totally accept myself. Happy?"

My older sister gave me a disgusted look. "You need to do the quiz at the end of the chapter. If you pass, you can move on."

Even practical Emmy was frowning at that statement. "So what if the readers don't? Do you give them a refund and recommend another book?"

Ashlyn nodded in agreement. "This does seem a little revenue limiting, Shel. Who are you to decide if someone is ready to fall in love?"

"I'm a licensed family therapist," Shelby replied tartly. "I'm not promoting unhealthy relationships here. I want people to be their best selves."

"Best selves," I repeated, finding the page with the quiz. "*When I look in the mirror I feel happy. True or False.* Sure, I can go with that, especially if I'm wearing a super cute outfit."

Emmy, however, wasn't done. "I think it would be wonderful if we were all our best selves when we fall in love but frankly don't you think that's a little...unrealistic? People fall in love every day in the middle of chaos and they manage to make it work. There's nothing wrong with working on yourself while you're in a relationship. If we did it your way, I think the species might actually die out."

"If people are coming to me for help, then I need to help them completely," Shelby argued, her pancakes abandoned. "I want them to love themselves."

"Maybe they can't see that they're lovable until someone else shows them," I replied, paging into Chapter Two. I've always been a bit of a rebel. Shelby was the rule follower. The true-false quiz was boring as hell anyway. Just a lot of new age self-esteem stuff. If my sister had her way, she'd have me meditating daily.

Ashlyn pointed at me, a big grin on her face. "That. That right there. Sometimes people have to be helped to see how amazing they are. It's great when people know it but that doesn't mean they should be disqualified from finding love. That's just mean."

I blinked, trying to remember my exact words. Something about not seeing they were lovable? I was so used to verbally sparring with Shelby I barely paid any attention to what I said. She was going to win. She always did.

Except this time might be different. Both Ashlyn and Emmy were nodding their heads and smiling and I couldn't help but feel like I'd said something very wise.

I had changed last night and it was awesome.

"Right I am, wrong you are," I said in my very best Yoda voice. "It's three against one."

"Fine," Shelby huffed. "Go ahead to Chapter Two. But don't say I didn't warn you."

Since I'd already delved farther into the book, I simply took another bite of pancake. Damn, they were good. Even food tasted better after a near death experience. At this rate, I was going to outgrow all of my clothes.

"Are you going to change the book?" Emmy challenged. "Let them know that while their best selves are ideal that doesn't mean they don't deserve love."

"I never say they don't deserve it," Shelby replied, exasperation in her tone. "I just say that they should work on themselves first."

"But they might misunderstand and think that you mean they don't deserve it," Ashlyn pointed out. "That's not a good way to endear readers to your book."

Shelby reached out a hand toward me. "Hand me the book

so I can make some notes."

"You wanted our help," I reminded her as I handed her the binder. "Now you have it."

"I agree," Emmy said. "If you want our help, we're going to tell you the truth."

"I want your help." Shelby had snagged a red pen from the end table and was frantically making notes. I had those pens all over the house and at school. "I really do. It's just this book is sort of special, that's all. It's like telling me my baby's ugly."

"You and Brad could never have an ugly baby," Ashlyn said, shaking her head. "You both have good genes. Now what's in Chapter Two?"

"Finding a man," I stated. "I've got that one covered. Just how many chapters are in this book?"

"Thirty-two."

Two down, thirty to go. That was a whole bunch of chapters.

CHAPTER TWELVE

Mia

MY PARENTS HAD come and gone, leaving behind a mountain of leftovers. They must have been cooking all morning, bless them. Emmy had an event that she was managing so she had to leave, although she didn't want to. Ashlyn had a niece's birthday party and she was ready to ditch it, but I managed to convince her to go. I wasn't going to do anything desperate while they were gone, for heaven's sake.

Shelby, on the other hand, couldn't be moved out of my house with a crane. We'd always been close growing up despite the age difference. She was such a mother hen I was surprised she hadn't married earlier and had a passel of red-haired kids but then I remembered how ambitious she was as well.

Don't get me wrong, my parents are fantastic, wonderful people but I had a bond with my sister that I didn't have with any other person on the planet. She might drive me crazy on a regular basis but there's no one else I would rather have make me insane than Shelby.

My dad was a stoic man who didn't show much emotion but he'd tried hard this afternoon. Mom, however, emoted all over the place, fussing and fluttering around me the entire time. She would have cut my pot roast if I'd let her. Heck, she might have even fed me, too. It was great to have so much familial love but I still wasn't thrilled about having people too close to me. A little fact I was having trouble explaining to my sister as my parents drove away.

"I'm just jumpy when people invade my personal space," I explained. "I'm sure it's only temporary."

Normally I was a person who hugged but today I'd had to grit my teeth and endure it. After last night I didn't want anyone too close. Not even Shelby. She was miffed about it.

"I hope so." Shelby was still watching out of the front window. "Because your target just pulled into your driveway. Dammit, we haven't had time to get a plan of action together yet. This is bad. Try to get rid of him."

"Target?" I echoed, scrunching up my face. I didn't comprehend what she was saying. "What target?"

She turned from the window and rolled her eyes. "Josh, of course."

Josh. What?

"He's here?" I jumped from my spot on the sofa that I had carefully guarded all day. I looked like death warmed over with no makeup and my hair pulled back in a ponytail. Shit, this was bad. "Why is he here?"

"I'm betting that Mom and Dad told his parents about what happened. They told him and...voila! He's here to make sure for himself that you're in one piece." Shelby tapped her chin and smiled. "Actually, that's a good sign. He didn't bother to call. He just came over on impulse. We can work with this. Now go put on some mascara while I stall your prince. Hurry!"

I dashed out of the living room and into the master bath, keeping one ear cocked for voices. I did hear the doorbell and Josh's deep timbre, although I couldn't make out what they were saying. Shelby would offer him something to drink and maybe even some of the food that my parents had made. Josh loved my mother's cooking, so it was a good bet he'd say yes.

I did a little more than mascara.

A tinted moisturizer, some blush, mascara, and a light lip gloss. I re-did my ponytail but this time with a fun clip that had some sparkle. I'd also changed out of my sweatshirt and into a cream-colored cotton sweater. The whole ensemble was designed to make me look good but not like I was trying too hard. It probably wasn't a good idea to let the *trapee* know that he was being lured toward a trap by an amateur trapper. Who still had thirty chapters to go.

By the time I returned to the living room, Shelby and Josh were chatting and laughing while he ate a sandwich. He had a beer in front of him along with a plate full of food.

Good job, Shelby. She'd kept him busy while I beautified.

He jumped up when I entered the room, his smile falling and looking more scared and concerned than I ever remember seeing him before. If I'd ever wondered if our friendship was real – and I never had – I wouldn't wonder now. No one could fake that sort of worry and fear. But could I turn that care into something more?

Probably not, but I was determined to try. I had to know one way or the other.

Rushing toward me, he wrapped me in a big hug. I stiffened instinctually, waiting for that overwhelming feeling of the walls closing in that I had been burdened with all day but it didn't happen this time. I didn't exactly melt into him but I didn't pull away immediately either. My head was whispering cautionary warnings but my heart was telling my brain to hush up. This was Josh and he wouldn't hurt me for the world. I could trust him and I made myself do just that, staying compliant in his embrace. I even managed to hug him back slightly, my palms resting on the firm muscles of his back. He felt warm and solid, like a wall of protection around me and when he pulled away I wasn't relieved.

He bent his head and brushed his lips against my forehead, a gesture he hadn't done since I graduated college. I remembered the day distinctly. He'd handed me a wrapped gift and then kissed my forehead.

"Thank God you're okay," he said softly in my ear, his warm breath caressing my flesh. I shivered but he didn't seem to notice the effect he had on me.

Story of my life.

"I'm fine," I assured him. "A little emotionally raw but physically I'm fine."

"Luke said that you had a gun pointed at you. Jesus—"

"She did but maybe we shouldn't rehash that," Shelby said loud enough for the neighbors to hear. "I mean…if she's not ready."

I'd already talked about it several times, first to the cops, then to my sister and friends, and then for my parents. I could do it again but I didn't really want to. It wore me out and made me think about things that were better left behind. I was all about the future now.

Feeling bold, I placed my hands on his chest and could feel the beat of his heart, strong and steady. To my surprise he didn't back away, letting them rest there as if touching him was an everyday occurrence.

"It was frightening. I did have a gun pointed at me and I was scared. I thought I was going to die but I was lucky. Both me and the clerk are okay. I just hope the police can find who did this."

The cops hadn't seemed like they were all that hopeful, though. It appeared that convenience store robberies were fairly common even in our boring little university town. The store hadn't had any cameras which shocked me and our eyewitness accounts were pretty vague. I had a feeling the only way these guys were going to be caught was if they were interrupted in the act of knocking over a store or perhaps turned themselves in directly to the police.

"You should have called me last night."

I couldn't think of one reason why I would have called Josh last night. He wasn't my boyfriend. We were indeed friends but I didn't make a habit out of calling him in distress, although there was that one time that I had a flat and didn't know how to change it. Shelby wouldn't have been any help.

"The girls were here."

I didn't know what else to say because it was the truth. Of course, my girlfriends were there for me. I would have been there for them, too.

A funny expression washed over his features and then it was gone. "I just hated hearing it from Luke, especially as you hadn't been returning my texts."

Really? He was going to bring that up now? I stepped back and my hands dropped to my sides.

"I got your texts last night. I was a little busy not dying. I'm sure you understand."

There were texts from earlier in the week as well that I didn't have a good excuse for but I wasn't exactly being rational at the moment. I was running on adrenaline and fumes, ready to crash at any minute. Josh just had the good luck to be here when I'd about had it with company. I suddenly wanted to crawl into bed and curl up into a ball.

"Of course, I understand," he protested, his cheeks red. "I was just worried. Turns out for a good reason. If anything had happened to you, I don't know what I would have done."

Shelby had been watching all of this without saying a word which was uncommon for my older sister. She liked to let people know her thoughts a good deal of the time.

"We all feel that way," she said, reaching out to touch my shoulder. She was respecting my need for space. "We all love her, don't we?"

Wow, she'd thrown down the gauntlet quick. No pussyfooting around here. Just put it out there and see how he'd handle it.

I should have known Josh wouldn't miss a beat. "We sure do. She's precious to all of us. What would I do without you to make sure all my history is correct? Or to taste test my cheeseburgers?"

You'd find someone else, jerk.

Josh wasn't talking about the same love that I wanted. He was all about our friendship. A word I was beginning to loath.

"You'd look it up on Wikipedia," I said, slowly falling into a soft chair. I was exhausted and all my non-sleep was catching up with me. "Looks like Shelby filled you a plate. You should eat before it gets cold."

He sat down again on the couch, for once looking unsure as to how to deal with me. Good. "Will you keep me company while I eat? I'd like to spend some time with you."

I tucked my feet underneath me and reached for the iced tea I had on the end table. That's when I noticed the binder wide open. I couldn't let Josh see it. That would ruin everything. Panicked, I quickly shut it but he had eagle eyes when he wanted to.

"Is that for school?"

Right. Yes. I'm a schoolteacher and that made perfect sense. Not that I was trying to trap a man, but that it was schoolwork. For students.

"It is. How's the food?"

"Fantastic. Your mother is an amazing cook."

"Someday I'm going to learn that recipe."

He took another bite out of the pot roast sandwich and then placed it back on the plate. "I just can't begin to tell you how relieved I am that you're okay. So many things ran through my mind when Luke told me the news."

Things? Like my dead body riddled with bullets? Since he didn't specify what thoughts he'd had I could only speculate.

"I had a few grim scenarios running through my brain as well. The whole thing probably lasted less than ten minutes but at the time it felt like forever. But I survived and now I want to concentrate on living my life."

He smiled, taking a drink of his beer. "That's a great attitude. You're a strong woman."

Being a wimp wasn't an option. Not with my sister and friends.

Shelby had been hovering around the perimeter somewhere in between the living room and kitchen.

"Another beer, Josh?"

He shook his head. "I'm not even halfway through this one. And by the way, congratulations on your engagement."

"You're coming to the engagement party, right?" she asked. "I got your RSVP. You and a guest."

Was she doing this on purpose? Reminding me that he had a girlfriend? The amazing Trisha.

Grimacing, he cleared his throat. "About that. It's just going to be me. My girlfriend and I broke up last night."

Trisha the Terrific was gone? What happened? Did I even want to know? Did it matter? Josh was single again and I was planning to make him fall in love with me. I only needed a plan and time to read this darn book.

Shelby and I exchanged a meaningful glance. I hadn't liked the idea of breaking up a couple but now the field was wide open.

Taking a seat next to me on the couch, my sister gave Josh a huge smile of delight. "I'm sorry to hear that, Josh, but I'm glad you're still going to come. It wouldn't be the same without you. And it will give you a chance to meet Mia's new boyfriend."

Hold on a second... What? My boyfriend? I didn't have one and Shelby knew that. What was she doing, and which chapter was this?

Clearly I needed to read ahead.

CHAPTER THIRTEEN

Mia

AFTER JOSH LEFT, I shut and locked the door behind him before whirling around to give my sister what I hoped was an accusing stare. She'd really stepped in it this time and damned if she didn't drag me with her.

"Are you out of your ever-loving mind?" I asked incredulously. "You told Josh I had a boyfriend. I don't have a boyfriend. I don't even have a guy I'm dating casually. For the last four months I've been in a virtual romantic desert and there is no oasis in sight. I'm fucked. Completely fucked."

Shelby waited until I'd run out of steam before speaking. "So much drama. You are not fucked. How are you fucked? I wouldn't have said anything if I thought it would be difficult to find you a man willing to take you to the party. That's the easy part, sis. Eligible men are everywhere."

I fell back into a chair, my arms and legs sprawled. "Only people who are already in relationships say that. I'm not falling for it."

"I already have a man for you," Shelby explained calmly. "Trent Aldridge. He's one of Brad's friends from college and from what I've seen is a nice guy. Good looking, successful. He'll be thrilled to take you to the party."

"What's wrong with him?"

Frowning, Shelby folded up the afghan I'd been using earlier. "Why would there be anything wrong with him?"

"He doesn't have a date."

"*You* don't have a date." She laid the afghan over the arm of the couch. "And there's nothing wrong with you."

"That we know of. I might have real issues and not be aware."

"I think we'd be aware by now," she replied serenely, retrieving her phone from her purse. "I'll text Brad to let Trent know that he's going to be your escort. I hope you two hit it off. He's the best man and you're the maid of honor, after all. You'll be spending a lot of time together."

It still didn't make sense. She might be able to get me a man at short notice but if she hadn't opened her mouth I wouldn't need one.

"Why did you do it? Why did you tell Josh I had a boyfriend?"

"Listen to me, Mia, because this is important." Shelby's tone had a sharp edge to it that garnered my attention. My sister didn't use it often. "Josh has to see you in a whole new way. He has to see you as a romantic partner and that means putting you in a boyfriend situation. We need to show Josh that you're someone that other men want. You're in demand."

"But I'm not," I pointed out. "Not even close."

"We're going to change that. By the end of the party, Josh's going to wonder how he never noticed how wonderful you are. Trust me."

I did trust my sister. For the most part.

"Seeing me as more than a little sister isn't going to make him fall in love with me."

"True," Shelby conceded. "But I have a plan for that. Seriously, you need to read the book. It's all in there."

"I will but I haven't had a chance."

"Good, because it's not enough to know what to do. You need to know why you're doing it."

"Okay, why are we showing Josh how desirable I am?"

Shelby grinned and slapped her thigh with excitement. "I'm so glad you asked. We're going to fire up Josh's competitive nature. It's in his DNA. He loves to win and you, my lovely sister, are the prize."

"You really have lost your mind. No man has ever fought over me. Heck, they haven't even fought over you."

"Tommy Baker almost did in high school. He tried to take a swing at Alex but he was too drunk to do it. They dragged him out of the party and took him home."

"Almost only counts in horseshoes, as Grandma used to say. Seriously, this whole thing sounds like something Grandma would tell us to do. Your theories are based in mid-twentieth century attitudes between men and women. How about some empowerment here?"

"There's plenty of empowerment in my book," Shelby replied dryly. "I promise you. And yes, I see what you're saying but some things really don't change. Men like to compete and they like to compete over women. I didn't make the rules, I only wrote them down."

I dragged the binder off of the end table and onto my lap.

"Just wait until Emmy reads this. She's going to have a cow. A big one. This sounds so old-fashioned and too much like a stupid movie on television. The make-him-jealous plot is as old as dirt, and might I remind you, it usually doesn't work very well."

"We're not making him jealous. We're getting him to want you because you're worthy of being wanted. That's different."

"A difference without a distinction."

Shelby groaned and pointed to the book. "You have to read it to understand. I make the point in the book that a woman needs to be sure that a man will step up and do the work in a relationship. As a gender, I feel that we are far too easy on men, but of course that's just my feelings. You need to make Josh do some of the work. Men don't appreciate things they can get easily."

I wasn't sure I liked where she was going with this.

"Are you calling me easy?"

Shelby sat up straight, leaning forward with her elbows on her knees. "Sis, I hate to tell you but there ought to be a bathroom wall with your name and number on it. *For a really easy, no stress relationship where you don't have to lift a finger, call Mia Kelly.* So I'm not saying you're sexually easy, but you are…easy. You're going to have to get tough. Look at me, for example. I don't put up with any crap from Brad and he knows it."

I couldn't stop the giggle that escaped my lips. "Did you send him a memo to tell him? I can see that."

Brad was a nice guy but he was always so formal and stiff. Like he had a broom handle wedged deeply in his anus. He was handsome, successful, smart, and devoted to Shelby. He just lacked a silly sense of humor, something that I absolutely had to have in a man.

"Will you take this seriously?"

I composed my features and cleared my throat. "Seriously. Yep, I can do that. So what's next, Coach? You're putting me in the game, but I don't have any strategy yet."

Folding her hands, Shelby gave me a smug smile. "That begins tomorrow. We have two weeks before the party and we'll need every spare minute you have. But first...you need to read the book. The whole thing. You've got to believe in the system if this is going to work."

Looks like I had some homework to do.

★ ★ ★

THE NEXT MORNING I was in the office early after a lousy night's sleep. Nothing that I wasn't used to but this time my head had been busy thinking about Mia.

What had happened to her.

What could have happened.

What kind of guy she was dating.

What screw I had loose that I was thinking about her all the time.

It was driving me crazy. I'd never obsessed about my friend like this and I didn't like it one bit. I'd almost lost her Saturday night and clearly it was messing with my brain cells.

By the time Luke showed up with two large coffees in paper

cups, I had a trash can full of wadded up paper that were once story ideas but now they were garbage. He placed a cup in front of me before lowering himself onto the couch in my office. I had parts of my storyboard everywhere and he had to gingerly tiptoe around it all because while it might look like chaos to him he knew I had a system.

"So did you see Mia yesterday?"

The coffee was halfway to my mouth when my brother asked the question and I smacked it back down to the desk.

"Jesus, is that all you want to talk about? Mia? She's fine. You could have called her yourself, you know."

Luke's brows shot up. "Who pissed in your Cheerios this morning? Damn, I only asked a simple yes or no question. When we hung up yesterday you were headed to Mia's house, so I thought the most obvious conversation opening was asking about that. You're a touchy bastard."

Groaning, I took a gulp of the scalding hot coffee, feeling it burn all the down my esophagus.

"I didn't get much sleep last night."

"Stop taking it out on people. This is one of the big reasons why you're single. You don't think about others."

That wasn't why I was single.

"I think about others."

"Of course, that's what you would say. Self-centered people don't often know that they're self-centered."

Was that the case? Was I self-involved and completely unaware?

"Fuck you."

My brother laughed and leaned against the desk. "That's

your answer to everything you don't like. Real eloquent, bro. That's another reason why you're single. You don't listen worth a damn. It's your way or the highway."

Now that I'd heard on multiple occasions from multiple people.

"If my way is better, why should I do it differently?"

"And you made my point exactly. Thank you."

"But that's not why I'm single. I'm single because I want to be. When I meet the right woman, I won't want to be anymore."

Luke shook his head. "You wouldn't know the right woman if she walked up to you and slapped you in the face with a fish."

A fish?

"I would know."

My brother just shook his head and took himself into his own office. Taking a sip of my coffee, I pondered his words, although I shouldn't have given them any more thought. He was just trying to piss me off but it wasn't working.

Would I know the right woman when I met her? I'd always been filled with confidence that I would but I hadn't realized Mia was a sexually attractive female until recently, so that didn't say much about my awareness when it came to the opposite sex. I might have already dated *the one* and didn't realize it.

Honestly, I wasn't even sure I believed in that *one* nonsense. The idea that there was one and only one person in the world that I could love seemed preposterous to me. It seemed rather more likely that a person met the one and fell in love when they were at a point in their life when they were ready to settle down.

Except that didn't make sense either because I had a slew of buddies that weren't looking for anything more than a roll in the hay and they were now happily – for the most part – married.

It was beginning to dawn on me that I didn't know shit about love. Or women. For a guy that had always prided himself on being savvy about romance, this was a startling conclusion. I might know a great deal about serial monogamy but I didn't know anything about a lasting relationship.

Supposing I wanted one of those, which I wasn't sure that I did.

My life was good. I didn't need a woman to be happy. I just needed my work, my family, and my friends. I was a lucky bastard to have so many terrific people in my life.

An image of Mia flashed briefly through my mind. It would good to remember what category she was in. Friend. Mia was a great *friend.*

I'd do well not to forget that.

CHAPTER FOURTEEN

Mia

I MET EMMY after work on Wednesday for dinner. As an event planner, the middle of the week was usually pretty dead for her and the best time to meet and catch up. We were going casual tonight, sitting in a booth at our favorite Italian restaurant. It was old, rundown, and a little cheesy with its red plastic tablecloths that perfectly matched the plastic flowers on the table. But the food was fantastic and the prices from the 1990s. Heavenly aromas wafted from the kitchen – tomato, garlic, and oregano – making my stomach growl loudly.

"I finished reading Shelby's book last night," I announced after the waitress dropped off our iced teas. "I have to say I'm impressed. No way could I ever write a book."

"I wouldn't have the patience. Or the time."

Emmy was a successful event planner who did weddings, anniversaries, bar mitzvahs, and the like. Since she was incredibly good at it, she was always in demand and booked up far in advance. It was only in the last year or so that she'd become rather picky as to what clients she'd take on. Otherwise, she'd be working a ninety-hour week or more. A bout of pneumonia where she'd ended up in the hospital had finally set her on a path to work-life balance. Last I heard, Shelby was trying to teach her to meditate.

A pretty brunette, Emmy always seemed poised and in control. Her life was planned down to the last second and she left very little to chance. She carried one of those tablet computers in her purse and that computer stored every detail about her life. Not that it needed to. Emmy had an amazing memory for details.

"So how was it?" she asked. "Just the usual stuff about loving yourself and sending positive vibes out into the universe?"

I hadn't been kidding when I told my sister that Emmy would have a cow when she read the book. Now that I'd read the book in its entirety I'd realized that only parts of it were…old-fashioned.

I couldn't think of a better word to describe it.

"It's a bit more practical than that. Actually, I was really scandalized at some of the earlier parts of the book. I told Shelby it sounded like advice from our grandmother."

Emmy rolled her eyes and sighed. "Let me guess. Don't call him, wait for him to call you. Don't be too eager. Don't be better than him at anything. Don't act too successful or too happy with yourself. Have I got it right?"

I had to laugh at my friend's cynical tone. "It kind of started out that way but then it took a turn I wasn't expecting."

Emmy's expression was dubious. "I'm listening. Go on."

I took a drink of my tea to give me time to gather my thoughts. I'd been thinking about the book all day whenever I had a moment or two to myself.

"I saw…a lot of myself in some of Shelby's cautionary tales.

I'm guessing that I'm the inspiration for her bad examples. Anyway, she doesn't say not to call a man because it's not ladylike. She says not to call him – and only in the beginning of a relationship – because we as women do too much of the work when we're dating someone. That we let men get away with murder. They don't have to lift a finger. She pushes the idea that we need to hold men to a higher standard, and if a man can't take one minute to send you a text or call you then he's not the kind of guy that you want."

I didn't mention the whole bathroom wall thing that Shelby had said. Her words still haunted me days later. Was I such a wuss when in a relationship? Apparently, my sister thought I was.

"I completely agree," Emmy said with a definite nod of approval. "Women let men get away with all sorts of shit when we really should be making them put in a little damn effort."

"According to Shelby if being easy on men were a crime, I'd be doing twenty-five to life."

Wrinkling her nose, Emmy's front teeth sunk into her lower lip. "Well...you do tend to make excuses for them. Not that we all don't do that from time to time, but that does seem to be your habit. Most of the men you've dated weren't worth a pile of spit, to be honest. You deserve better."

I did deserve better. Funny how a near death experience puts a hell of a whole lot into perspective. I wanted a man who was as invested in the relationship as I was. I wanted him to love me as much as I loved him.

It wasn't too much to ask.

"I deserve better," I echoed, smacking the table with my

hand to emphasize my point. "And I will get better. You know, from now on, I'm not going to take any shit from a guy. If he says he'll call the next day, he better do it. In fact, he better do everything he says he's going to do. Because that's what decent human beings do, right? They keep their word."

"Good for you. Go get 'em, girl. Show them who is the boss." She was about to take a drink of her tea and then stopped. "You are, in case that wasn't really clear."

"Damn right I am. I'm not the same person who walked into that convenience store. I'm a strong woman who doesn't need a man in my life to be happy."

Emmy's brows shot up in surprise. "So if Josh doesn't man up and act right, you'd end the relationship?"

"We don't have a relationship."

"But if you did," she persisted. "Would you end it? If he didn't keep his word? If he acted like a jerk?"

The one thing the book had shown me was that love without trust and respect wasn't much of a prize. If the only way I could have Josh was to be his doormat...

I'd pass.

"I would end it." I could hear Emmy's sharp intake of breath. "If Josh can't be a decent boyfriend then he doesn't deserve me."

"I'm proud of you."

I was proud of me, too.

"I can't keep making the same mistakes and expecting a different outcome. If Josh is the type of guy who only takes and never gives, then yes, I'd kick him to the curb."

Sadly, I didn't think I was ever going to have to make that

call, though.

ON SATURDAY I didn't go to the office, instead heading to my parents' home to help my dad with repainting the back porch and steps. It was just one item on my father's to do list for winterizing the lawn and house. At his age, he didn't need to be out there all day working when Luke and I were around to help him. Except that my brother was nowhere to be seen.

"Where is Luke?"

My dad stacked the paint cans on the porch. "He called to say he had to go into the office. It's just you and me."

"Bullshit, I'm the boss and there's no reason he needs to work today. He just doesn't want to paint."

My dad just shrugged, an act he wouldn't have done twenty years ago. He'd been one hard ass about household chores and no one in our family got to skip them because they had *other things to do.*

"There's plenty of work to be done. He can do the house lights for the holidays."

That was a crappy job, cold and sometimes snowy, too. Luke could climb up on the roof and risk his neck hanging lights and putting the Santa by the chimney.

We worked side by side for a while just talking about all the other items on Dad's list. It was never-ending from what I'd seen but I liked the fact that he'd always been proud of the way our home looked. Every year he had two lists of projects – one for summer and one for winter. Light bulbs barely even had a chance to burn out in our house before he had them replaced.

After we finished the first coat of light blue, we retreated to the garage where Dad put on the small space heater and then grabbed two beers from the refrigerator. He handed one to me before settling into a lawn chair. I took the one next to his facing the street so we could watch the comings and goings of the neighborhood. Dad had left up the garage door and this was one of his favorite things to do in between chores. He said people didn't care about their neighbors anymore. They only thought about themselves and their phones.

Hell, he was probably right. He was most of the time anyway.

"Dad…can I ask you a question?"

I'd been debating the wisdom of asking this question since we'd started painting and had come to the conclusion that it was a stupid idea, but I couldn't seem to stop myself. My conversations with Luke and Rachel had me all twisted around. Then Mia getting caught in that robbery… I barely knew which way was up anymore. All I knew was that I had more questions than answers in my life.

"You know you can always ask me a question, son. It sounds like you're bothered by something."

That pretty much summed it up. Something. What I didn't know.

"How did you know Mom was the one? I mean…how did you know that you wanted to marry her and spend the rest of your life with her?"

If my dad thought the question was strange or unexpected he

didn't act like it. In fact, he didn't even hesitate to answer as if he'd been waiting for the moment I'd finally ask.

"I know this isn't want you want to hear but you just know. When not being in the same room with her brings on an actual physical pain, you know. When you admire her and want to brag to all your friends about her, you know. When you don't care if her hair isn't washed or if she's wearing makeup, you know. When she's the first person you want to see in the morning, you know. When she makes your life better by just being in it, you know."

That's it? That's the entirety of my father's wisdom on love and women. I would just know?

Shit.

"No offense, Dad, but that sounds like a load of bull."

Luckily, he didn't take offense, simply laughing at my statement and taking another gulp of his beer.

"I told you it wasn't what you wanted to hear. What did you think I was going to tell you? That you'd hear music like in the movies? That'd be nice but I doubt it's going to happen. Why are you asking? Do you think you've met someone?"

"No, but Luke said I wouldn't recognize the right woman if she came up and slapped my face. Rachel says that I keep breaking up with them because I have to do it first. I don't like being dumped."

I didn't mention the whole Mia situation. Suddenly finding her sexually attractive didn't have anything to do with this problem. That was a problem all on its own.

"No one likes being hurt, although you may have gone out of your way to avoid it. You won't be able to forever, though.

No one can. Eventually you'll get your heart broke just like the rest of us mortals." Dad sat straighter in his chair and turned his gaze to me. It was that look he'd given me when he was dropping me off at college. That *you're a man now* look and *I'm about to lay some wisdom on your ass, so listen up*. "You're a good son, Josh. Funny, smart, and a hard worker. No one could be more proud of you than your mother and I."

There was a "but" coming... I could feel it.

"But..." I prompted.

Dad laughed and shook his head. "There is no but. You've grown into a fine man. Your mom and I did a damn good job."

It was nice that they could congratulate themselves.

"It sounded like there was a but in that sentence."

"I just wish that perhaps you would have had to work harder for some things. Women being one of them. It's come far too easy for you. You don't appreciate what you have and you think it will always be that way. If you had had to struggle a little more you might not act like this, breaking up with them before they break up with you. You could avoid heartache because there was always another woman to take their place. I'm sure you've had fun but I don't think it's done you much good as a person."

I wasn't sure what to say. My father had rarely spoke so open and honestly with me about love and relationships.

"You think I've had it easy? That I don't appreciate the women in my life?"

For a moment I thought he was going to deny it but then he nodded. "Yes, I do."

Wow, I was floored, barely able to take a breath. I couldn't blame Dad, though. I had asked and he'd answered.

I didn't know what else to say but once again my dad was right there for me.

"The question, son, isn't how you know when you've met the right woman. That's not the important point here. The question is...what kind of man do you want to be with a woman? Any woman, not just the one. That's the real issue, and only you can answer that."

I didn't have an answer. I wasn't even sure what he meant exactly.

"I want to be like you."

Shaking his head, my dad took another drink of his beer. "No, son. That's not how this works. You can't be an imitation of me. You have to be a genuine you. You've been so busy working on *what* you wanted to be you haven't given a moment of thought to *who* you wanted to be. Maybe now's the time."

I couldn't think of anything I wanted to do less. I had a good life and this discontent was just a phase. Tomorrow or the next day I'd forget all about it. Everything was fine and I didn't need to find some mythical woman of my dreams. I was letting other people get into my head and mess with my brain when I should be focused on what was important. The work.

For once, Dad was wrong. I knew who I was.

And I wasn't about to change for some female.

CHAPTER FIFTEEN

Mia

THE DRESS I was wearing cost way too much money but Shelby had assured me that the expenditure was worth it. She'd also told me that she and Brad were going to pick up the tab for the bridesmaid dresses and groomsmen's tuxedos. When I'd heard that I almost passed out in relief. One item off of my "to be paid for" list.

The sleeveless dress was a soft gold silk that fell just above my knees. It was a clever design that made it look like a skirt with a top but it was actually one piece and very comfortable. My favorite part was the pearls around the neckline that seem to glow under the lights. I'd paired the dress with gold sandals and jewelry, even putting a small butterfly clip in my updo.

I didn't often feel confident or beautiful but when I'd looked into the mirror tonight I'd been happy with the reflection that stared back at me. I felt sophisticated and a little glamorous, which was a far cry from my usual workday attire.

I'd enjoyed the admiration that I'd seen in my date's eyes tonight. Trent Aldridge was everything Shelby had said he would be – so far, anyway. He was handsome and successful, a full partner in his family's law firm. He was tall and knew how to wear a suit, too. He was unnaturally tan for this time of year, his golden skin showing off his dark blond hair and blue eyes. From our brief conversation it sounded like he'd just come back from vacation at a tropical destination.

"I'll get us a drink," he offered when we arrived at the fancy hotel that was hosting the engagement party. Normally Emmy would be working feverishly to make sure everything went off without a hitch but Shelby had insisted that their friend turn all responsibilities over to her assistant Jana. "What would you like?"

It was a special occasion and that called for a special drink.

"Thank you. Champagne would be lovely."

"I'll be right back."

Trent strode across the room to the bar area. No, he strutted. That was definitely a strut. I could see from his expression that he was enjoying the eyes on him. Interesting. I'd already figured out that he had more than his share of self-esteem. I'd also found out that he didn't have much of a sense of humor. I'd sort of been joking around and all I got in response was a frown. It wasn't about religion or politics, so I hoped I didn't upset him but dammit, it was funny. He should have laughed.

Josh would have laughed.

Josh isn't your escort this evening. Get over it.

My gaze instantly sought out the man that I was supposed to hunting...or trapping...or whatever. Tonight was about him seeing me in a different light, a romantic one. Trent was a good sport to play the part of the besotted suitor but I still couldn't shake the idea that there was something really wrong with him if a good-looking guy with oodles of money couldn't get a date. It didn't seem plausible. Shelby had said that he just broke up with a girl so there might be an excellent explanation.

Josh.

He was wearing a dark blue suit with a matching silk tie. As sexy as Josh was, he never seemed quite comfortable all dressed up. He was more of a jeans and t-shirt kind of a guy but he did look good. Unfortunately, he didn't look thrilled to be dressed in his Sunday best and his shoes shined to a mirror-like finish. Even his curly hair had been tamed tonight with a smattering of gel.

Our gazes clashed across the dance floor and for a moment I thought he was going to come speak to me but then Trent showed up at my elbow again bearing a fluted glass of golden liquid. After seeing Josh, I needed a drink. My knees were trembling and I was having trouble catching my breath. I accepted the glass from Trent and took a generous sip, allowing the cool elixir to run down my suddenly parched throat. It wasn't fair that one man had this sort of effect on me.

Trent grinned, showing off a set of white teeth that would have made a shark proud. "Is that him?"

"Him?" I echoed, still watching Josh on the other side of the room. He was now chatting with Ashlyn who looked lovely in royal blue. "What do you mean?"

"The guy. The one I'm supposed to be making jealous tonight. I know all about it."

Oh, he did? That was news. It sounded like I needed to have a talk with my older sister, especially if she thought that throwing around my personal business to practical strangers was a good idea.

Dragging my gaze away from Josh, I finally looked up at my

date. "Just what is it that you think you know?"

"There's a guy you like and you need me to make him jealous. Don't worry, babe. I've got it covered. He'll be wishing he was me before the night's over. If he already doesn't, that is."

Yep, a healthy ego on this one. Why on God's green earth would Josh Henry be jealous of Trent? He was just as successful and just as handsome. He also knew when to laugh at a joke, which was far more important than looks.

And did he just call me *babe*? WTF? I was beginning to see why good old Trent didn't have a date.

"You don't need to do anything," I assured him, not sure what this guy had in mind. "We'll just have a good time tonight. Don't worry about him."

Trent reached for my glass which I wasn't happy to give up, but I didn't want to make a scene. He placed it on a table and then grabbed my hand, pulling me towards the dance floor.

"The fun starts right now. Let's dance."

A guy who danced couldn't be all bad. I just might enjoy this party.

★ ★ ★

Josh

MIA WAS DANCING with her date who I had learned from Ashlyn was Brad's best friend and soon to be best man. How convenient. The maid of honor and the best man. It would have made a cute movie.

"Mia looks amazing tonight."

Luke had sidled up next to me, a bottle of beer in his hand.

As usual, he looked like he didn't have a care or worry in the world. He'd never admit it but he loved getting dressed up and going to parties, although he pretended to hate it. Every chance he could get, he had Rachel putting on her dancing shoes and attending some sort of fundraiser for charity.

"All the ladies look lovely this evening."

I sure as hell wasn't going to admit that I'd been watching Mia for most of the night. She did look incredible tonight in a gold dress that showed off her shapely legs. Legs which were currently on the dance floor with that guy. I'd been told his name was Trent and he was far too good-looking and smooth. I'd gone to college with guys like that who had too much money and not enough sense. He certainly oozed confidence and that appeared to be attractive to several of the women here but to me he looked arrogant as shit. Mia could do better.

"I wasn't talking about all the women. I was talking about Mia. What's the problem? Don't you think she looks gorgeous?"

Finally turning to look at my brother, I saw the smirk that I was expecting. He was enjoying this.

"I do."

"And she's not our little sister, either."

"No, she's not."

"So there's no reason to feel guilty about how attractive we find her."

"We?"

Luke took another draw from his bottle. "Well, me in a completely innocent happily married man kind of way and you in a…probably much less innocent single guy way."

Luke had no idea the thoughts I'd been having about our

former neighbor, and he wouldn't hear about them from me.

Trent's hand strayed down and brushed Mia's pert rear end. Fuck no. But then maybe it was just an accident. That could happen. Sometimes a guy didn't know where to put his hands–

Shit, the asshole did it again. That was no accident. Just some smarmy jerk who thought he was God's gift to women. He was whispering something in Mia's ear that had him grinning but Mia didn't seem to think it was entertaining. She wasn't smiling which was highly unusual.

I'd been watching this for too long. I'd had enough. I was literally hot under the collar, my neck red with anger. Trent needed a break from dancing.

With a growl, I shoved my bottle into Luke's free hand. "Hold my beer."

Striding toward Mia and her date, I could hear my brother laughing and saying, "I love those words. Something fun always follows."

Let's hope I wouldn't end up as part of the Darwin Awards after tonight.

CHAPTER SIXTEEN

Mia

HANDSY. TRENT WAS getting far too handsy and if he touched my ass cheek one more time I was going to break those fingers that were wandering too far from where they should be. All the while, he was telling me about how much money he had and how successful he was. His breath had the distinct odor of whiskey and I was betting he'd had more than one. He was, frankly, full of himself. Shelby was going to get an earful about this tomorrow. If she was ever planning to fix me up on a date again, she'd better do her homework first. This night was heading for an iceberg.

A man who danced wasn't worth all the crap I was dealing with.

So it was real relief I felt when Josh tapped on Trent's shoulder to cut in.

"Do you mind?"

Trent looked like he wanted to say no, which was insane because by his own admission this was what he was there for...to get Josh to want to intervene. Not that I fooled myself that Josh was jealous. He probably was just being polite. We'd danced at my parents' twenty-five year anniversary party, too. I remembered that night like it was yesterday. I was a gawky teenager and Josh had been like a prince, leading me around the dance floor despite my lack of grace. Hopefully I'd improved in the ensuing years.

Trent let go of my hand reluctantly. "I suppose one dance is okay. I'll see if Brad wants to have a drink."

Goody, more alcohol. That should improve his personality.

Pulling me into his arms, Josh glanced over his shoulder at Trent's retreating figure. "I only just met that guy but I already don't like him. But maybe that's just me."

Laughter bubbled from my lips at his sardonic tone. "Well, at least you're open-minded about it."

"It's just that he really doesn't look like your type."

The music was soft and slow, and Josh's fingers were pressed into the small of my back, sending all sorts of tingles up my spine. He smelled delicious and I had to fight the urge to press my face to his jacket and inhale deeply. The warmth from his body scorched my skin through the flimsy silk of my dress and I wondered if I could see that flesh right now if there would be a physical mark. A reminder for later when I was all alone and we were tucked up in our separate beds.

Remembering that Trent was supposed to be my boyfriend, I couldn't say that he wasn't my type in the least. That he was a jerk and the evening couldn't end soon enough. Shelby had got me into this mess but now I had to keep up the charade.

"Really? What would be my type?"

I wanted to hear his answer. It would say a great deal about what Josh thought about me.

"Not that guy. I guess I pictured you with someone who

is…nice. I never thought you'd go for someone so obvious."

"Obvious?"

"Looks and money." Josh cast another glance sideways to where Trent and Brad were making a toast with some of their other friends. "I would have bet you'd be the type to want someone deeper than our friend over there."

This was fascinating. Clearly Josh thought I was nice and deep. Not a bad combination, unless he was looking for a woman opposite of that.

"What about you?" The question was out before I could zip my lips firmly closed. "What's your type?"

It was an asinine question because I already knew. I'd seen him with too many women to count over the years.

He hesitated, his steps to the music slowing slightly almost as if he didn't want to stumble while he thought of an answer. His palm pressed into my back and he leaned down to whisper in my ear.

"Can we get some air? It's getting hot in here."

Boy howdy, I couldn't agree more. With every brush of Josh's body as we'd moved across the dance floor my arousal had spiraled higher and higher. If we'd kept it up I might have melted into a puddle at his highly shined shoes.

Letting him lead me out of the party, I caught my sister watching us out of the corner of my eye. She raised her champagne flute in salute as we went by and I almost turned and stuck out my tongue. Suddenly this whole man trap plan seemed far-fetched and wholly out of the question.

But I've changed. I go after what I want now. I can't keep sitting back and hoping for something that will never happen. I have to be proactive. I have to be a woman of action.

It was the *how* that I was unsure about. I wanted Josh but I didn't want to trick him into falling for me. I wanted him to do it because of who I am.

This must not have been Josh's first time in this hotel because he'd found a lovely glassed-in room that was perfect for this time of the year. Closed in so the cold wouldn't get to us, but open so that we could see the stars. It was quite romantic. There wasn't another person in sight. Just the two of us and we sat down on a loveseat, his thigh brushing against mine. Luckily, I'd had literally years of practice being this close and not showing how much I wanted to reach out and touch him.

My heart pounded so loudly I was sure he could hear along with everyone else in the hotel, including the parking valet out front. I didn't want to sweat in this very expensive dress but it was sheer torture waiting for him to say something. Anything. The tension between us had never been this thick.

"Ever since that robbery you were in I've been thinking about you. What if something bad happened to you?"

Slowly exhaling to calm my jangled nerves, I did the unthinkable. I reached out and placed my hand on his. If I wanted him to see me in a new light, then I had to do things I didn't do before.

He didn't pull his hand away. To my utter shock, he laced our fingers together, holding on to me tightly. My chest tightened painfully and I could barely take a full breath. So full of emotion at that moment, I had to blink back the tears that I absolutely couldn't let him see. I was fully prepared for Josh's friendship, even his indifference. But this tenderness was something that I'd never expected. His expression was tortured with thoughts of what might have happened. I couldn't say that I too hadn't been plagued with bad dreams of what might have been but I hadn't expected this.

"But I'm fine. Nothing did happen."

I wanted desperately to tell him that I'd changed but I wasn't sure he'd understand. Josh had always gone after whatever he wanted without hesitation.

"But something could have. What would I do without you? You and Luke are my best friends."

A lump lodged itself in my throat and I couldn't reply. I wouldn't know what to say so it might be for the best. Josh and I had grown closer as the years had gone by but not once until this moment had he ever referred to me as his best friend, equating me with his brother.

Bittersweet. That's how it felt.

Sweet that he had such deep feelings for me. Bitter that they were the wrong ones. I wanted his love but I would have to settle for his friendship. Overcome by the tension between us, my own heart cracked open, spilling almost thirty years of emotion that I had bottled up so he would never see. Lips trembling, I opened my mouth to tell him just how much he meant to me. How much he would always mean to me.

I had no idea how I'd kept it a secret all of this time. Every cell of my body was urging me to tell him the truth, tell him how much I loved him. How I'd loved him for years and could he ever feel the same for me? If there was ever a time to spill my guts it was now, when his hands were holding mine so tightly as if I might disappear if he let go.

Raising my head to admit the feelings that I'd been hiding I was quickly silenced by the sheer emotion etched in the lines of his face. He'd been torturing himself with images of the worst-case scenario. Without thinking, I reached up and laid my palm on his cheek as a way to soothe the tumult I could see in his blue gaze. I was here and I was okay. That's what we needed to concentrate on.

His cheek was slightly rough under my fingertips. Josh had shaved before he came but already he had a slight shadow on his jaw. I couldn't stop myself from caressing it even though I didn't have any business doing so. That was for women like Trisha the Terrific, not Mia the best friend.

I tried to speak again. "Josh, I—"

I didn't get any further and I didn't care. Josh's lips had crashed onto mine and we were kissing as if our very lives depended on it. My fingers threaded in his hair, soft and silky and in contrast to his stubble-roughened cheek. His tongue ran across my bottom lip requesting access and I didn't think twice, granting it immediately. This was my dream come true.

Shelby just might have a bestseller on her hands if that stupid book worked for everyone the way it had worked for me. I was officially out of the friend zone as of now. Hallelujah. I swear I could hear angels sing as our lips pressed together and our tongues played a sensual game of tag. The temperature in the room had soared and I was probably beginning to sweat through my dress shields. I didn't care. A dress was a small price to pay.

As quickly as it had begun it was over.

Josh raised his head, his expression...shocked? Scared? Dumbstruck? I couldn't tell exactly but it wasn't the blissed-out reaction that I was hoping for. My own euphoria was quickly dissolving as the reality of it all was washing over me. He wasn't happy about what had happened.

"Jesus, Mia. I'm sorry…shit…I shouldn't have done that."

Wrong. You should have done it years ago.

What was I supposed to say? Act like it was no big deal? Inside I could feel my heart shattering into a million tiny pieces but there was no way I was going to let him know. I would walk away with a little bit of dignity. Somehow.

"Then why did you do it?"

The turmoil inside had the words coming out more aggressively than I'd planned and Josh blanched, finally releasing my hands and backing away a few inches. The steamy temperature that had surrounded us just minutes ago had plunged and I shivered from the cold, rubbing my arms where goosebumps had risen.

"I–I have no excuse. I shouldn't have taken advantage of you like that."

I wasn't in the mood to be magnanimous. It was like I'd been plunged into a bathtub full of icy water.

"You didn't answer my question. Why did you do it then?"

He shook his head whether to deny that he hadn't answered my query or to say that he wasn't planning to answer.

"I'm really sorry, Mia. I was way out of line."

Okay, it was the latter. He either didn't know why he did it, or he did and he wasn't talking.

Moonlight, stars, a pretty girl. Was Josh that shallow?

"I guess I was just an amusement in between girlfriends."

I wanted to hit out and hurt him like he'd hurt me. Hey, I'm not proud of it but I'm only fucking human and I was bleeding to death here. My chest cut open and my heart ripped out and stomped on a few thousand times. I was going to kill Shelby and her stupid book because this was far worse. To have a taste of what it could be like and then lose it…

It was a nightmare.

"No. No, not at all." He was shaking his head again, the color high in his cheeks. "It was…shit, I don't know. You look so beautiful tonight, Mia, and I kept thinking about losing you…"

"So you kissed me?"

I stood then, not wanting to prolong this fruitless conversation. His words were not making it better.

Scraping his fingers through his dark curls, he sighed heavily and looked down at the floor.

"It feels like I don't know what I'm doing lately. Please forgive me, Mia. Yell at me. Slap my face and call me names. But please, I don't want to lose you."

A woman can only take so much and I was exhausted. Loving Josh was wearing me out. I needed a break, if only to the bar for a strong drink. Maybe several.

"Josh, you've never had me to lose."

Then I turned on my stiletto and walked back to the party with my head held high. Josh could break my heart but he couldn't break my pride. It was about all I had left.

CHAPTER SEVENTEEN

Josh

"*J*OSH, YOU'VE NEVER *had me to lose.*"

Mia's words echoed in my brain along with the sound of her heels against the marble floors as she walked away. From me.

I'd acted like an idiot and I didn't have any explanation for my behavior. Mia hadn't been unreasonable in asking for one but I truly didn't know what had compelled me to kiss her. I could blame the robbery and the thought of a gun aimed at her chest but that would be a lie. I'd already started thinking of her differently even before that happened if I was being completely honest. That incident had just sent my emotions into outer space. Normally I was cool and in control but tonight with Mia I was a blithering buffoon, unable to verbalize any of the myriad of emotions swirling in my gut.

All I knew for sure was that I'd realized that I'd taken Mia's friendship for granted for far too long and that I needed to show her my appreciation. A kiss hadn't been planned. It had been an impulse. An amazingly pleasurable impulse, and if I had any ideas of going back in time and viewing Mia as just the kid next door that was shattered when my lips met hers. Mia was a grown woman and I was hyperaware of that suddenly.

How do we be friends now?

I'd meant it when I said that she and Luke were my best friends. But I was sure that sticking my tongue in a friend's mouth was going to cause issues. I'd tried to apologize but maybe the real problem was...

I wasn't sorry.

Sue me, but I'd enjoyed it. The only reason I'd stopped was because it was Mia. She wasn't a female I had any right to kiss. Christ, she was here with a date. A guy I couldn't stand but if she liked him then that was all that mattered.

I clearly had issues dealing with Mia being a friend and also a woman I was sexually attracted to. Common sense would probably dictate that I break off the friendship but that was not going to happen. That left me one option. Get over it. Stop drooling over her and straighten up. I'd ignored Mia's female allure for a couple of decades; surely I could do it again. Maybe I could find a lovely woman and ask her to dance. The world was full of possibilities. All I had to do was look farther than the house next door.

Feeling much better and full of resolution, I marched back into the party determined to find a distraction, whether blonde or brunette. I'd apologize to Mia as well and mean it this time. I didn't want to ruin what we had. It was too good. If she asked me again why I'd kissed her I'd simply say that she looked so lovely I couldn't help myself. It wasn't far from the truth. We'd talk it out like we always do and everything would go back to the way it was before. I'd promise to behave and she'd accept my apology. Mia was good like that, so forgiving. Which might explain why she was here with that douchebag named Trent.

When I entered the hotel ballroom I didn't see Mia but I did see her friend Emmy also entering the party. I made a beeline straight for her, cornering her next to a carving station.

"Have you seen Mia?"

I'd always had a feeling that Emmy didn't have a high opinion of me and tonight was no exception. Her smile fell and she appeared to not want to answer. In fact, I was sure she was going to tell me to shove off when she finally replied. "Not lately. She left the party for a few minutes and then came back. She was dancing with Trent last time I saw her."

The thought of Trent touching Mia didn't sit well with me at all. He was such a jerk. I could see it as clearly as the back of my own hand. I'd gone to school with assholes like that and he wasn't fooling me for a second. He wasn't good enough for Mia, although I couldn't think of one man that was. I sure as hell wasn't. Not that I was looking to be her guy, because I wasn't. I wouldn't ruin our friendship over a temporary fling.

"I need to talk to her."

"She's having fun, Josh. Why don't you just leave her alone?"

I didn't have time to explain. "I need–"

Emmy rolled her eyes and waved away my objection. "Yes, yes, we all know it's all about you. Do you even care about Mia? Because she's having a good time tonight and she doesn't need you to find little tasks she can do for you to make your life easier."

"Little tasks?" I repeated. What in the hell had Mia been telling her friends? "What are you talking about?"

Emmy's lips twisted in distaste. "You need Mia to help with

your video games. And you need Mia to help you pick out Christmas and birthday gifts for your family. You need her to help you pick out wall paint and furniture and I think she even helped you pick out your car, too. Leave her alone, Josh. It would be kinder if you did."

With a huff, Emmy turned and walked away, making her the second woman who was pissed at me tonight. A personal record and one I was not proud of. I honestly had no idea what Emmy was talking about, but I did get from her that perhaps I wasn't as thankful for all that Mia had done for me. My dad had said I was spoiled and it was looking like he wasn't the only one with that opinion. Was I that much of a jerk? Was it really all about me? I needed to take a long look at myself, no matter how painful it might be.

It was time to leave this party. I was angering each guest one by one and that needed to stop. Emmy thought I wanted to ruin Mia's evening and that wasn't the case at all. I'd go home and call her tomorrow to apologize. The night had not gone the way I'd expected and it would be far better to cut my losses.

Stopping briefly to let Luke know I was leaving, I headed for the exit. My brother hadn't tried to convince me to stay but I'd be getting a phone call early tomorrow morning for all the details. He'd want to know what was going on and then he'd give me his absolutely not asked for opinion about it all.

As it was a Saturday night, the foyer of the hotel was busy. The bar was off to the right and it did a brisk business on the weekends. For a moment I slowed by the entrance, thinking I might go in and grab a much-needed whiskey but that would only mean I'd have to call a cab to get home. I'd had one and a half beers and two was my limit when it came to driving. I could have as much alcohol as I wanted when I got home.

I passed by the alcove that led to the restrooms and caught movement from the corner of my eye. It was Trent and Mia, and the bastard had her by the arm while she was struggling to pull away. A red tide washed in front of my eyes and the frustration of the entire night came to a head. Any other time I would have thought it through but not tonight. The kiss. Mia. Trent. Emmy. It had all been too much.

I stomped over to the couple and grabbed Trent's wrist. The one that was attached to the hand holding onto Mia. I squeezed as hard as I could until he let go and Mia staggered back, rubbing her arm. If she had a bruise there tomorrow, I was going to kick this little shit's ass from here to Chicago and back.

"What the fuck are you doing?"

Spittle flew from Trent's mouth and landed on the carpeted floor. His face was red and quite unattractive. Not so much the rich playboy at the moment. I cast a quick glance at Mia to make sure she was okay.

"Are you alright?"

She nodded, still rubbing her arm. Her eyes were bright with tears and that just pissed me off even more. This guy was scum. "I am. I just want to leave."

That was fine with me.

"I'll take you home."

Trent stepped forward, swaying on his feet and reeking of whiskey. What kind of shape was the rest of the wedding party in? "The hell you will. She's my date."

More spittle, more red face. I had no fucks left to give. Every ounce of my body was screaming out to protect Mia. She wasn't going to spend another minute with Trent.

"Just walk away. Don't make this worse than it already is."

Of course, Mr. Daddy's Money couldn't keep his mouth shut. Or his fists to himself. He took a swing at me, awkward and ill-timed because he was obviously inebriated.

This wasn't my finest hour.

So I punched him. Right in the jaw. Trent stumbled back and then fell on his ass because he could barely stand up. I didn't hit him as hard as I could have but it was enough. He'd feel it tomorrow and that was the plan. He needed to think about what he'd done.

Mia's eyes were wide and she was staring at me as if she'd never seen me before. I don't think I'd ever hit anyone in her presence. I slipped her hand into mine and tugged her away from a complaining boyfriend. Trent was still lying on the floor bellyaching about how unfair it all was. I leaned down to say one last thing.

"Just a word of advice. Don't manhandle women like that. And whatever you do, don't you ever hurt Mia. Do you understand?"

A small crowd had gathered around us and I had a feeling I knew what was next. The cops. I didn't really want to be around when they showed up, although he had swung first and was clearly in the wrong. I hurried toward the exit, now glad that I hadn't valeted the car.

For once, Mia was silent as we left the hotel. I bundled her into my car and pulled onto the road that would lead to the main highway. Neither one of us had said a word.

"You want me to take you home?"

To my surprise she shook her head. "I'm not ready to go home yet."

I'd just drive until I figured out where to go.

CHAPTER EIGHTEEN

Mia

FIGHTING AN INTERNAL war with myself, I sat next to Josh in the car. Angry and hurt didn't even begin to describe my emotions and they were too complicated and jumbled for me to make any sense out of them. I wasn't even sure why I'd allowed him to lead me out of the hotel except that the last thing I'd wanted to do was stay there. Now we were driving down the road together and my conflicted self didn't know whether to jump from the vehicle or stay where I was. I was leaning toward the latter as the outside was cold and the car was warm.

I'd told him I didn't want to go home and he'd accepted that answer. We weren't headed for my condo or his place, either. I didn't know where he was going to take me but I trusted him.

I know, I know. Why should I trust him after what he'd pulled in the solarium? I was incredibly devastated by Josh backing away but that was one moment in decades of otherwise trustworthy behavior.

His actions in the last hour had infuriated and exhilarated me in equal measures. Pulling away after our kiss had broken my heart but his intervention when Trent had been a drunken dick was far different. I'd never seen Josh punch anyone, let alone hit a guy because he was hassling me. It was out of character for the man that I knew. Just like that kiss. He certainly wasn't himself tonight.

The drive lasted quite awhile and I had no idea where we were going until we were there. Josh turned down the long dirt road and a million memories flooded my mind all at once.

The lake. All those lazy summers that I had thought would never end.

Our families had come here so many times when we were young. Picnic baskets stuffed full of food, including my mother's famous fried chicken. There had been inflatable pool toys, sunburns, and then when the sun went down, a bonfire and marshmallows. Such innocent fun and the images were so clear I could feel the warmth of the sun on my face, smell the coconut tang of suntan lotion. I could even smell the acrid smoke from the fire and taste the sweet stickiness of the s'mores. I would give anything to go back to that time just for one day. Back when my worst problem was freckles and whether Shelby would eat the last hot dog. I didn't know how good I had it until I grew up.

My already shattered heart ached for that little girl, so innocent and naive. She had no idea what she had ahead of her. The good and the bad. Such amazing highs and such horrendous lows. If I could give her some advice I'd tell her not to worry so much. Have fun with her friends and eat the chocolate. But most of all I'd tell her not to accept anything but the best from the people in her life. Don't settle for okay or mediocre.

Josh parked the car in the same place our parents always had, under an awning of oak trees. They'd grown larger since the last time I'd seen them, although only their outline was visible in the moonlight. The trees were a few feet from the two familiar picnic tables and the sandy shore of the lake. The headlights skimmed over the surface of the water, completely calm and serene. I was so used to the laughing and running around that it was strange to hear nothing but the crickets singing. There were no people, and I'd bet even the squirrels were asleep. Josh and I might as well have been the only two people in the world.

But we weren't and there was unfinished business between us. I had so many questions but didn't have a clue how to ask them. He was like another person tonight and I wanted to know why.

So of course, I was the first one to speak, filling the void with words. A neutral topic that wouldn't make the tension between us any worse.

"I haven't been here in years."

"I think the last time was my high school graduation party. I wasn't even sure I could still drive back here, to be honest. I'm surprised they haven't made this a city park with a gate."

We were speaking so softly as if someone might hear us.

"What made you come here?"

The silence stretched on so long I didn't think he was going to answer, but he did.

"I don't know. It wasn't a conscious decision. I was just found myself driving in this direction. I guess I wanted to go someplace where we were always happy." He'd been staring straight ahead but now he turned to me, unclipping his seatbelt. His features were shrouded in shadow, making it impossible to see his expression. "I didn't mean to be such an ass tonight, Mia. The fact is I don't know what the fuck I'm doing most of the time these days. I've always been working toward a goal but now...? I just don't know. My dad says I'm spoiled. Fuck, I probably am. I just don't know what the hell I'm supposed to do or be. Do you ever feel like that?"

Sometimes truth hits a person right between the eyes, waking them up to reality. This was one of those times. I'd put Josh on a pedestal for so long I'd forgotten he was only human like the rest of us. I think perhaps many of us had though, including Josh. He was beating himself up about something so commonplace, yet he thought he was the only one.

"All the time," I answered. "Practically every single day. But I think I've figured out why life makes us feel that way. If we didn't, we might not try harder. We might get complacent and simply float through our days. I don't think we were meant to do that."

"When did you get so wise?"

I smiled in the darkness, knowing the exact moment life had come into sharp focus for me.

"When I had a gun pointed at my heart. That will straighten out your priorities quick. I was just going through the motions before that moment, half asleep. I can't go back to who I was before."

"I liked her. There was nothing wrong with her."

I shook my head, although I wasn't sure he could see in the darkness. It was strange how the lack of light made it easy to talk like two kids in a blanket fort with nothing but a flashlight, except all we had was the moon and the dashboard.

"She was fine but she simply sat back and waited for life instead of going after what she wanted. I won't do that again."

"So what is it that you're going to do or go after? What do you want that you didn't have before?"

The million-dollar question. I'd give him the two-dollar answer. Heaven knew I couldn't tell him that he was my prey, although right now that game seemed very far away.

"Love. On my terms."

I could hear his chuckle over the engine and the heater. "You weren't ever going to get it with that asshole."

I actually kind of felt sorry for Trent. He would forever be known now as *that asshole* or *that douchebag*. Shelby and Brad had probably heard the story – or at least Trent's version of it – by now and they were going to have to pick sides. What a fucking mess.

"I know. He was…practice."

It was the best explanation I could come up with. That tension that I'd felt in the solarium of the hotel was back but this time it was a thick wall between Josh and me. Each one of us on our designated side.

"He was a jerk. You could do a hell of a lot better."

"Yes."

There would be no arguing. I wanted peace between us and besides, he was right. I was so tired, bone deep. My plan to get over Josh hadn't worked and my plan to make him fall for me wasn't working either. I wanted… Shit, I didn't even know what I wanted. Peace. Tranquility. Someone to hold me at night and tell me I'm pretty. Apparently, that was all too much to ask for.

"I don't know how you ended up with a guy like that–"

"Stop," I commanded, laughing at his tone. "Just let it go, okay? He wasn't that important. He never was."

My palm itched to smack Josh. He couldn't see what was right in front of him. He was important, not some jerk of a guy.

"He hurt you."

Rubbing the spot on my arm where Trent's fingers had surely left a bruise, I nodded. "Just physically, and it will fade. You need to let it go."

It was then that I remembered that I hadn't thanked Josh. I could have held my own. Trent wasn't the first guy to think he was owed something after a few drinks, but the chivalry was nice. It was so rare these days.

"Thank you. He was getting ugly. I was about to take off my high heel and hit him with it."

"That might have improved his looks." Josh shifted in his seat turning his body towards me. "How can you just let this go? Doesn't it piss you off?"

Unbuckling my own seatbelt I also turned to face him, stretching my legs slightly and kicking off my uncomfortable heels. The heater vent blew directly on my knees, fluttering the skirt of my dress, and making the car toasty warm despite the chilly temperatures outside.

"I'm not letting it go. Shelby and Brad are going to hear all about this, and can I just say that I'm not thrilled about my sister marrying a man who has friends like Trent. I will also give Trent an earful the next time I see him, which might be the rehearsal dinner for all I know. But he will hear from me about his behavior. But I have to tell you that he's not the first guy to get handsy or try something."

"I'm not sorry I hit him."

"I'm not sorry either."

Laying my head against the seat, I listened to the hum of the engine. Josh reached down and flicked on the radio.

The oldies station. Perfect for our walk down memory lane. My eyelids grew heavy as the sounds of the eighties drifted over me. After everything that had happened, I needed about a week of sleep. I was just about to drift off when I felt Josh move. I didn't bother to open my eyes, assuming he was going to buckle his seatbelt and drive me home.

When he touched my face, it was unexpected. My flesh sizzled where his fingers brushed my cheek, tucking a strand of my hair behind my ear. My lids wanted to open but I firmly kept them shut, not wanting to see his face, if I even could in this light. He was only being kind and that's not what I needed from him. If I kept my eyes closed I could pretend for a few minutes that he hadn't battered my heart and tossed it away earlier.

"Mia."

He was so close I could feel his warm breath when he spoke. I had begun to tremble, not from the cold but from the heat that was coursing through my veins. I was debating the wisdom of opening my eyes when I felt the touch of his lips on mine. Tentative at first and then more demanding when I didn't push him away. He tasted of beer and bad decisions. This was a horrible idea and I'd regret doing it, if not right after then sometime very soon. But my heart was already in ten thousand pieces, so what else could he do to me?

Except make me feel desired.

His hands cupped my cheeks as he deepened the kiss. My own fingers rested on his chest and I could feel his racing heart under my palm. He was as affected as I was. He might deny it or say he didn't mean it, but he liked it. I liked it too and I wanted more.

I wanted it all.

CHAPTER NINETEEN

Mia

OVERLOAD.

It was the only word I could use to describe all the sensations coursing through my body all at the same time. The tiny voice in the back of my head that was currently questioning my sanity had to be quelled so I knocked it out, placed a sack over its head, and dragged it into a closet, firmly closing the door. I locked that sucker too and then put a chair under the doorknob. I couldn't be too careful. I'd waited literally years for this and my shattered heart was fully in charge. Maybe I'd let the little bastard of common sense out of the closet…later.

Right now all I wanted to do was feel. Josh's fingers glided up my thigh and for a moment my universe tipped and spun.

Josh had his hand under my skirt.

It was better than any of my fantasies because it was real.

It shouldn't have been a surprise, though. Going after what I wanted was far better than sitting at home dreaming.

Hot. It was so hot in this vehicle. The windows were fogged up just like when I used to go parking in high school. Then the expectation was far more innocent. Kisses and maybe some wandering hands. If I really liked the guy I might let him put his hand under my sweater.

I wanted these clothes off. A sheen of sweat covered my flesh and Josh's and I pulled at the neckline of my dress, trying to cool off the overheated skin. I could taste the tang of salt under my tongue when I pressed my lips to the cords of his throat. Even with the sound of the radio, I could hear our ragged breaths and gasps as lips and fingers found sensitive spots. Unerringly, Josh nipped and kissed the base of my neck where the pulse beat madly, sending shivers of arousal straight to my curling toes. His hands had lifted my dress and exposed my thighs, his fingers stroking what he'd uncovered.

Still going up in flames, all I wanted to do was toss aside my dress and that's what I did, tugging it over my head like an old t-shirt instead of the pricey frock that it was. It landed on the seat next to me as Josh slid the driver's seat all of the way back and pulled me onto his lap, straddling his legs.

Our hands never stopped moving, almost frenzy-like in their urgency, as if someone had been holding us back and had finally let go. It was probably true for me but I didn't know what Josh's story was, only that he couldn't seem to get enough of me, which I sure as hell wasn't going to complain about. Just as I'd imagined, he knew his way around a female's body and didn't think only of himself. Most guys might have pushed a girl to her knees by now, but Josh slid those clever fingers inside my drenched panties to work some of his evil magic.

Wet and slick, there was no resistance when a thick digit slipped inside of me. I gasped when he added a second, throwing my head back and moving my hips in time to his small thrusts, desperate for satisfaction.

"Christ, Mia. So fucking tight."

I barely registered his words and I couldn't have replied even if I tried because right then he started a thrumming motion on my clit with his thumb. My nails dug into the muscles of his shoulders and my entire body stiffened. Crying out his name, I tumbled over into the abyss but Josh was there to hold me as I fell. Riding his fingers until the very end, my forehead fell onto his shoulder as the waves ebbed. So good.

But not quite enough. I was greedy and I wanted more.

My fingers fumbled with Josh's belt buckle and his hands clamped down on mine. At first, I thought he was pushing me away but then I realized he was trying to help me. In his haste, though, he wasn't making any of this easier. Both of us panting like we'd run a marathon, we managed to undo the belt, his trousers, and pull down the zipper. Eager, I reached down and ran my fingers down his hard cock, reveling in the feel of it and drawing a tortured groan from this man that I had fantasized about for so long. There were so many things I wanted to do to him but this would have to suffice for the moment. Impatiently, Josh jerked down the front of his boxers, freeing his dick from its cotton prison.

Hot, hard, and impressive, but velvet to the touch. His cock was long and thick and I shuddered with anticipation thinking about how amazing it was going to feel deep inside of me. Running my hands up and down the shaft, I smiled when he moaned, his hips bucking upward sending me an all too clear signal. He was more than ready and frankly so was I. There was only one tiny detail. That voice in the closet was screaming now through the gag and I had to concede it might have a point.

"Condom?" I asked, my thumb swiping over the head of his cock. He trembled and hissed, his grip on my hips tightening.

Josh always placed his wallet on the dash when he drove. He said that he didn't like to sit on it so retrieving the foil square wasn't as difficult as I'd imagined. Not thinking too deeply about what in the hell I was doing, I helped him roll the condom onto his cock and spread my legs a little wider. My damp skin stuck slightly to the leather of the seats making a loud, out of place sound and I froze for a moment, holding my breath, but if Josh noticed he didn't act like it. Distracted, he was already pushing the straps of my bra down to bare my breasts, his fingers teasing the rock hard nipples.

Positioning myself over his cock, I sank slowly down, feeling every inch of him until he was into the hilt. Not moving, I savored the feeling of being so full, my walls clutching him as if my very life depended on his invasion.

"Josh."

I said his name like a prayer, if only to assure myself that this was really happening. After all this time, Josh was as deep inside of me as a man could get, and it was better than I ever could have imagined. Neither one of us said a word, but our bodies began to move in a rhythm as old as time. Thousands of years ago, a man and a woman might have been on this exact spot doing this exact dance.

The interior of the vehicle must have been a hundred degrees and our sweat-slicked bodies slapped together as I rode his cock, pressing my clit against his groin with every thrust of his hips upward. This was no gentle coupling, two tender lovers exploring each other's bodies for the first time. We were fucking each other like animals, pawing at the clothes we hadn't bothered to shed if only to bare a few more millimeters of flesh.

Josh bit at my shoulder, surely leaving bite marks I'd need to hide the next day but I paid him back with the nail marks on his shoulders and arms, red half-moon shapes that would mean long sleeves for a week.

The one thing neither of us would be able to hide was our expression of pure satisfaction. Others might see our smug smile but only we would know what it truly meant.

The coil of arousal in my belly had tightened painfully and I was teetering on the precipice of my orgasm, almost afraid to let go. I didn't want this to end but I couldn't hold back forever. This march was inevitable and when Josh dipped his head and closed his mouth over my nipple, his teeth scraping the tender bud, the game was over.

I went off like the fireworks on the Fourth of July. Stars and white lights flickered behind my lids and the world seemed to speed up on its axis. Josh followed me over, an expletive on his lips. Teeth gritted and jaw tight, he thrust up one last time, his grip on my hips punishing. There would be bruises there tomorrow as well, although covering them wouldn't be an issue. His head fell back against the seat and the cords of his neck stood out in stark relief against the smooth golden skin.

There had never been a more beautiful man, of that I was sure. Seeing him like this was worth the wait.

When it was over, we collapsed together in a tangle of sweaty limbs and sticky clothing. Sucking air into my aching lungs, I stole a glance at Josh. His eyes were closed and his breathing ragged and labored. The reality of my current position and situation was slowly seeping into my pleasure addled brain.

I'd just ridden Josh like a pony. No, maybe more like a bronco rider but thankfully it had lasted far longer than eight measly seconds.

I was half-dressed and my makeup probably resembled a Picasso painting by now. My bra was pushed aside and my boobs were hanging out. The soaking crotch of my panties had been shoved aside and Josh's cock was still inside of me.

I'd vigorously fucked Josh in the front seat of his BMW sedan.

And I didn't regret it.

However, it might prove to be the dumbest thing I'd ever done. I had a feeling that I was going to find out very soon.

CHAPTER TWENTY

Mia

WHOMEVER WAS BANGING around in my kitchen would soon be dead. Of course, I knew good and well it was my sister Shelby. There was no way I could walk out of her engagement party last night with Josh and not get interrogated this morning but I'd sort of thought she might sleep in. One glance at my phone told me that it was seven-thirty in the morning and I hadn't fallen asleep until four. Three and a half hours of rest wasn't going to do much for mood nor my appearance.

There were no messages from Josh either. That wasn't going to help.

Dragging on a robe, I padded on bare feet from the bedroom to the kitchen where my sister was making coffee as loudly as she possibly could. A passive-aggressive alarm clock dressed in yoga pants and a sweatshirt.

"If you break my coffeemaker you're buying me a new one."

Shelby jumped and placed a hand on her chest. "You scared me to death."

"I scared you? You've got nerve. You broke into my house. I'm the one that should be calling 911."

"I have a key to your house. It's hardly breaking in."

"That's for emergencies."

"Is there any bigger emergency than you leaving with Josh last night? I heard he decked Trent. What in the hell happened? I only heard Trent's side and might I say he sounded a little shady. Brad had to talk him out of calling the police and pressing charges."

I could only imagine the story the little weasel told Brad and Shelby. One where he was the poor put upon victim and Josh was the big bad wolf. Screw him.

"He deserved it. In fact, he's lucky I didn't do it myself because I was getting ready to smack him with my high heel." Shelby's eyes were round as she pulled down two cups from my cabinet. "Let's just say he thought I owed him something for pretending to be my boyfriend. Charming friends your fiancé has. In no way does he deserve the title of best man, and I won't be doing anything with him at your wedding other than keeping my distance. What a tool."

She poured two cups and I accepted mine gratefully, adding cream and sugar before taking an experimental taste.

Ahhh. There was nothing like that first sip of the day. I could almost feel the caffeine start to whiz through my veins like a racecar at Le Mans.

"I'll talk to Brad about Trent. I'm sure he has no idea his friend is like that with women."

Plopping down on the couch, I set my coffee on the end table. "I bet he knows, he just probably doesn't think it's a big deal. Boys will be boys and all that. I'll bet you five dollars that Brad defends his friend and says that I blew this entire situation out of proportion."

Shelby came to sit next to me, tucking her legs underneath her and leaning back on a large cushion.

"Brad would never do that."

I held out my hand. "So it's a bet?"

Narrowing her eyes, she took my hand and shook it. "Fine. You're very cynical today. So what happened last night?"

A half smile curved my lips. "We went to the lake."

"The lake?" Shelby echoed. "What lake? There isn't a lake around here."

Sometimes I worried about my sister. She was the smartest person I knew but she had zero memory about the past.

"Charlotte Lake," I explained. "Where we used to go when we were kids."

"I haven't been there in years."

"Neither have I but that's where he took me."

My sister's gaze ran from my toes to the top of my head. "Did you go swimming or something?"

Laughing, I shook my head. "Of course not. The water would have been…oh, about fifty degrees. I'm not a polar bear. At first we just talked."

"Talked?" Her brows shot up. "Wait…at first?"

I could feel the heat rising in my cheeks. "You had your engagement party last night. Shouldn't you be lolling around in bed with Brad this morning?"

"Brad had a flight to New York at six so I've been up since four. He and I have a lifetime to…loll, as you put it."

"That's the most unromantic thing I've ever heard. He just left this morning?"

"He had an important meeting. Life doesn't stop just because I'm getting married. Now let's get back to you. What did you do after you talked?"

There was no avoiding it. I'd tell her eventually because we told each other everything.

"Josh and I...had sex."

I couldn't call it making love because we'd gone after each other like beasts in the front seat of his car. I was pretty sure I had a bruise on my lower back from the steering wheel hitting me there with every thrust of Josh's...

Like she'd been touched with a cattle prod, Shelby sat straight up, slopping coffee on her sweatshirt.

"You went back to Josh's house and had sex?"

"No."

Her mouth fell open and her gaze drifted to the hallway that led to the bedroom. "Oh my God, is he here?"

We could do this all day but I decided to end her misery.

"No. Listen to me. Josh and I had sex. In his car. Then he brought me home and left. He is not here. If he was, I'd have been pushing you out of the front door."

She kept brushing at the coffee on her shirt. "I don't understand."

"We had sex in his front seat."

Saying it made it sound incredibly awful. Cheap and tawdry. That made me cheap and tawdry too, which didn't help my mood. Luckily the coffee was kicking right in.

Shelby leaned forward, her hands wrapped around her cup. "How? I mean...logistically..."

For fuck's sake, that's what my sister was concentrating on

here?

"We were very determined."

That wasn't a lie, either.

Rubbing at her temples, my sister let out a loud sigh. "Maybe you should start from the beginning."

Always the therapist.

"How far back do you want to go? Childhood? Or just last night?"

"Let's start with the party and work forward."

How did it all start? Right…he'd asked me to dance and it all went south from there.

★　★　★

Mia

WE'D POURED MORE coffee and I'd told my sister the entire story with most of the detail. Emphasis on *most*. The really juicy stuff I kept to myself but she definitely got the picture.

"And he just dropped you off here and didn't say anything?"

Shelby sounded scandalized for me but I was fine with it. Actually, I was glad he hadn't felt the need to fill the shocked silence with a bunch of words that he may or may not feel the next day.

"What did you want him to say? Marry me and have two point five kids and a dog? He made sure I was okay and was very sweet. I didn't invite him in, either. I think both of us needed some space after what had happened."

"So what are you two now? How do you go forward? Has he called?"

I held up my cell phone which right now might as well be a paperweight. "No messages. I checked when you woke me up. As for what we are now and how we go forward? I don't know. Our friendship has taken a turn. It might be destroyed."

"And you're okay with that?" There was disbelief in my sister's tone. "What if you never see Josh again?"

It wasn't a huge town that we lived in. I would see Josh again at some point. The only question was in what context?

I'd given this a lot of thought last night after he'd dropped me off. It was the reason I hadn't fallen asleep until four.

"I'll be fine," I assured my sister. "I don't regret last night. I know you probably think I do or that I should, but I don't. I wanted it to happen. I had ample opportunity to back out. He didn't push. I walked past the line of our friendship with my eyes wide open and I'm glad I did."

"I am so lost right now. Clearly, you threw out my book and went off the path."

Not in the least.

"It was your book that helped me. Don't you see? It was your words that convinced me that I don't need to accept anything half-assed anymore. If Josh doesn't feel the same, then I have to move on. He either wants to try a relationship with me or he doesn't. Full stop. I have to stand up for what I want and I might lose him in the process. I'm okay with that. He's not the one if he can't make the effort."

Shelby looked at me with new respect. "Um...wow. It's hard to believe that my little book has done all of this. But I have to say that I hope you and Josh can work this out. What if he doesn't call?"

I'd thought about that.

"He'll call. I don't know when but he will. He hates situations that don't have closure. He'll call if only to tell me that he doesn't feel that way about me."

"What will you say?"

"I'm going to tell him the truth. Most of it, anyway. I won't tell him how I've been in love with him since I was a little kid but I will tell him that I have romantic feelings for him and that I want a relationship."

Shelby was shaking her head. "Sis, don't do it. You're giving him way too much power over you."

"No, he had way too much power before but not now. After what happened that night at the convenience store I'm completely awake. I can see things that I didn't before. I deserve better than some guy's smallest efforts."

"But you had sex with him."

Boy, did I ever. Sweaty, bang your head on the roof of the car sex.

"I did. Now there's no more wondering what it would be like. I can move forward if it doesn't work out."

"And hate his guts."

"It's a good thing you decided to write nonfiction because your storytelling skills suck. I don't think hating someone is a happy ending." I sighed, not sure how to explain it. I barely understood it myself. "Listen, I'll be sad if Josh doesn't want to try. Really, really sad. I'll have to take time to mourn because it will be like a death of a dream. But he's not to blame here. I'm the one that built all of this in my head and heart. I won't hate Josh. I might dislike him for a while but I won't hate him."

"I will."

I patted her hand and chuckled. "I appreciate that. Now I really need a shower. Are you staying?"

"I'm not leaving you when you need me. We can go out to brunch or something."

Food and socially acceptable morning alcohol. It was exactly what I needed while I waited for Josh to get his head out of his ass and call.

CHAPTER TWENTY-ONE

Josh

TUGGING NERVOUSLY AT my t-shirt collar I stood on Mia's front porch. I'd barely slept after dropping her off here last night, my mind going over and over the events of the evening. What had happened and all the alternate paths that we could have taken.

If we hadn't danced...

If I hadn't kissed her in the solarium...

If I'd been a few minutes later or earlier and not seen that asshole manhandling her...

If I hadn't driven us to the lake...

If I hadn't kissed her again...

If she hadn't kissed me back...

That last one was the big one, although I was under no illusions as to whose fault this was. It was mine. I'd started it weeks ago when I'd realized that Mia was gorgeous, sexy, and wonderful. I'd thought I could keep it under wraps, pretend that it was all the same but it wasn't.

I hadn't even consciously driven her to the lake last night. I'd simply wanted to take her someplace where we'd both been happy and carefree, so I ended up there.

Then I'd fucked her viciously in the front seat of my car. I was never, ever selling this vehicle.

I hadn't even been romantic or sweet about it. I'd pawed at her like a man let out of prison after twenty years, although to give Mia credit she'd given as good as she got. I was covered with nail and teeth marks under my clothes. Still it wasn't the way a man made love to a woman the first time. There had been no candlelight or prelude. Hell, there had barely been any foreplay but she'd been hot, wet, and ready just the same. So fucking tight, too. Shit, I was getting hard standing right here at her front door just thinking about it.

Mia had surprised me. I hadn't expected the tigress that lurked under the quiet history teacher exterior. It was hot and very sexy that she was just so naturally good in bed. Or in a car. I'd been dogged last night with visions of fucking her all over town, every night club and movie theater. Her head thrown back, her red hair in a tangle around her shoulders, her skin glistening with sweat. Clearly, I needed deep therapy.

She's my friend. Now she's my lover. Could I have both? Did I want to?

I had to be realistic. I sucked at relationships and I didn't know shit about love. Hadn't my brother and Rachel just told me that a few weeks ago? If I had to choose, I'd want her as my friend. Lovers come and go. Friends are forever.

Which was why I was standing here at her front door on a Sunday morning holding a giant cinnamon bun still hot from her favorite bakery and two coffees. I'd almost turned and left when I'd pulled in front of her home though. A vehicle was parked in her driveway and it looked like Shelby's car. Had the sister heard about all of my sins? I was about to find out.

I knocked and waited, my heart in my throat. I was having second, third, and fourth thoughts about this but we needed to talk. I hated feeling like we were in limbo and I was terrified of losing her from my life. She really and truly was my best friend other than Luke. I'd meant what I said.

The door swung open and Shelby stood on the other side, looking surprised to see me. With one glance I knew that she knew and my face grew warm as her gaze ran from the Styrofoam tray of coffee to the white box that housed the cinnamon roll.

"Josh."

"Shelby."

"You punched Brad's best man last night."

And I'd do it again. In fact, I still may if I ever see his smug face around town.

"I did."

"He told me that you were drunk."

"He was confused. He was the one that had had far too many."

"Mia told me that he was getting handsy."

"He was hurting her. He deserved what he got. I won't apologize. Your fiancé has shit taste in friends, by the way."

I must have said the magic word because the door opened wider and Shelby stepped back to let me in.

"That's exactly what Mia said. Do you want to come in?"

"Please." I looked around the living room but Mia was nowhere in sight. "I need to speak to Mia."

"She was taking a shower. I'll go get her." Shelby sniffed the air. "A Figaro's cinnamon roll? Are you in the doghouse?"

I wasn't sure but I wasn't taking any chances. While Shelby disappeared down the hall, I went into the kitchen to set down breakfast, noticing that there was already a half-drunk pot of coffee. Mia and Shelby had to have been awake for awhile. Maybe Mia had slept much better than I had. A fact that sort of pissed me off. How could she be so cavalier about what happened last night? Wasn't it as big a deal as it was for me?

Fuck. Then it occurred to me that perhaps it hadn't been a big deal because it hadn't been...good. For her. Mia had rocked my world but she might have thought I was mediocre at best. I'd thought she'd liked it by all her moaning and breathy little cries that were sexy as hell but guys could be fooled. I didn't want to think she'd faked it to save my fragile male ego but it was a possibility.

Now I was really pissed off. I didn't need a woman coddling me, pretending to enjoy sex when she really didn't.

"Hi."

Whirling around, I saw Mia standing there wearing jeans and a sweater, her long hair pulled back into a ponytail. Her features were composed and it was hard to tell if she was glad or mad to see me.

"Hi." I made a weak gesture to her kitchen table. "I brought some breakfast. Figaro's. Your favorite."

The Mia before last night would have squealed in delight and grabbed a fork. We didn't even bother with plates, the two of us just eating out of the box. It was obvious I was fucked when she didn't move, although her gaze flickered toward the coffee and roll.

"That's very thoughtful. I am hungry. You even brought coffee, too."

The tension was back between us but not like last night. This was far worse, uncomfortable and damn awkward. I didn't like it and I just wanted things to go back to the way they were. Turning back time, however, wasn't an option. There was only one way through this and that was to slog forward. Shit.

"We need to talk."

She nodded. "Give me a minute. I'll tell Shelby I'll meet her at the restaurant. We were going to have brunch."

Mia turned and went into the living room. I heard a few muffled voices and then the front door. She returned and sat down at the table, lifting a cup from the tray.

"So let's talk."

I'd planned every word I was going to say but damned if I could remember any of it. What was I supposed to do now?

Stall. Stall and eventually I'll remember. Better yet, get her to talk. Find out what she's thinking and feeling.

Swiping two forks from her kitchen drawer and then settling into the chair opposite her, I flipped open the lid and the yummy scent of vanilla and cinnamon assailed my nostrils. Normally this would have been a comforting aroma to me but the smell of food at this crucial juncture in my life was making me slightly sick to my stomach. If I messed this up...

Holding out a fork, I waited for her to take it and dig in. There was a moment's hesitation but then she did.

"I won't eat too much since I'm meeting Shelby in a little while."

Apparently I was on a clock, although I didn't know exactly

how much time I had. Might as well just do this.

"Mia, I've been up all night thinking about what happened last night—"

"Let me stop you right there." She held up her hands, the fork dangling from her fingertips. "I've been thinking about things too and I think we should just simplify this and cut to the chase."

I was all for that.

She leveled her gaze on me, our shared breakfast forgotten. "Josh, do you or do you not want to have a romantic relationship with me?"

CHAPTER TWENTY-TWO

Mia

WAITING. THAT WAS the hardest part.

I'd found the courage to ask the most important question and now the ball was in Josh's court. He either wanted to be with me or he didn't. Either way, I was going to be fine. It might take time but I'd come to the fork in the road. I couldn't stay on this path any longer, wishing and hoping for something that might never happen. It was better to know. It might be more painful, though.

It was a simple yes or no question but Josh appeared to be having a great deal of difficulty getting one of those words out of his mouth. His face was red and his hands were gesticulating wildly in the air, all the while trying to speak. Not wanting to clue him in to the turmoil inside of me, I stayed very still and quiet in my chair. This was a task he had to complete on his own.

He finally managed to spit out some words.

"I don't understand."

Hmmm....he was stalling. It wasn't a good sign and my heart sank into my stomach. The answer was no. He just didn't want to say it. I'd never thought of Josh as a coward but at this moment he wasn't being the most courageous man I'd ever known.

"Yes, you do. It's a simple yes or no question. Do you want to try to have a romantic relationship with me?"

He opened his mouth and then snapped it shut again. Another bad sign. Looks like I'd be meeting Shelby for brunch quite soon.

"It's not that simple."

I wasn't letting him off the hook. It actually really was that simple and clear. Last night was either just a casual shag or it meant something. Which was it?

"I think it is." It wasn't easy keeping my voice even when my throat was closing up with emotion. I'd cry later and maybe scream and stomp my feet but there was no way in hell I was going to let Josh see me like that. Not in this lifetime. "You either have feelings for me or you don't."

"Of course, I have feelings for you, Mia. We've known each other practically our whole lives."

That was the problem.

"Do you want to date me? See where this goes?"

He was rubbing the back of his neck and I could swear sweat had popped out on his forehead. He was nervous. Well, so was I.

"You're my best friend. I don't want to lose that."

That was a no, and it was as close as I was going to get out of him.

"I'm disappointed in you, Josh. Of all the people in my life, I didn't think you'd turn out to be the chicken shit one. Just say what you mean. You don't have romantic feelings for me."

He looked like he wanted to run for the exits. "It's not that—

I just– Shit, Mia. This is complicated. Whatever happens I don't want to lose you from my life."

I looked at Josh, really looked at him. It was strange that I could see all of his imperfections so clearly now and still love him. If anything, it made him more endearing and far more human. But I was done waiting and living on hopes and dreams. I needed to take back my life and this moment was a huge step in that direction.

Steeling my nerves, I placed the fork on the table and then flipped the box that held the cinnamon roll closed. Standing, I picked up the box and held it out to Josh.

"I think it's time for you to go then."

He stood as well, accepting the box, a dumbfounded look on his face. "What? I don't understand again."

"Then you need to pay closer attention." I pointed to the front door. "It's time for you to go. I'm not going to settle for maybe or so-so. I'm not someone's side piece or dirty little secret. If we had a one-time casual thing then I'm fine with that. I have no regrets. But at this point you either want to give us a try or you don't."

"It's not like that. You know how I feel about you."

I shook my head, keeping my resolution strong. I could easily wilt and give in. A small part of me wanted to.

"Actually, Josh, I don't."

Turning on my heel, I walked toward the door, hoping that he was following me. It was time for him to go.

"Please don't be upset," he pleaded but he was indeed following on my heels. "I don't want us to be angry with each other."

"Then you're in luck. I'm not mad or upset. My life has

become so clear to me these days. I can't sit back and let life happen to me. I have to take control. I'll call you when I'm ready to be friends again. Until then, I'd appreciate it if you'd back off. And before you ask the question, no, I don't know how long that will take."

In another time I might have been happy to see how horrified Josh looked. This...he hadn't expected when he came over today. I couldn't help but wonder what he had thought would go down. Maybe he'd say that last night was a mistake and I was supposed to agree. Then we'd simply go on pretending it never happened.

Fat chance of that.

"I can't leave like this." There was desperation in his voice but I wouldn't allow myself to be moved. I had to stay strong or I'd be right back where I started. "We have to work this out."

The truth will set you free.

I'd been hearing that saying my entire life. It was time to see if it was really true. I was about to make Josh understand just what in the hell was going on.

"I can't do this anymore," I said, opening the door for him. Deep inside I could feel my heart pounding painfully against my ribs. This was the scariest thing I'd ever done in my life. I was terrified. It was like jumping off a cliff without a parachute. There was nowhere to go but down and the fall was a doozy. "I have feelings for you. I don't just want to be your friend. I want to be more than that, and I have for a long time. I can't live on dreams and unicorns anymore. If you can't return those feelings then I need to find a way to move on. I deserve better than this."

Josh blinked a few times, his jaw working as if he was going to say something but no sound came out. I waited, my hand squeezing the doorknob until my knuckles were white. His eyes were dark and his face pale, no sign of his usual easygoing smile.

I'd shocked him. He really didn't have a clue. Not sure if that says more about him or me. Either way, he was not sweeping me into his arms.

This wasn't a romantic movie and suddenly music was going to start playing and we'd both end up kissing and crying, vowing eternal love. That shit didn't happen in real life and it sure as hell didn't happen to me.

Without another word, Josh slipped past me and bounded down my front steps toward his car. The vehicle that less than twenty-four hours ago had been the site of our steamy assignation. And yet that same passionate man who had left marks on my body from his lovemaking was hightailing it out of my condo community right at this moment.

I closed the front door and went back into the kitchen, picking up the abandoned coffee. Still hot. I took a few sips and then tossed it down the sink, the beverage only serving to make me nauseous.

This was the end of a huge part of my life and it hurt. I hadn't expected it to be this physically painful but it felt like someone had ripped my heart from chest with a pair of pliers. No anesthesia.

But it was also a new beginning, a new chance. My entire future was spread out before me with a myriad of possibilities. Where do I begin?

Picking up the pad and pencil I kept next to the refrigerator, I began to make a list. I needed a plan.

What I want for my life.

CHAPTER TWENTY-THREE

Josh

I DIDN'T HAVE any particular destination in mind when I left Mia's house but I ended up at my brother's. Honest to God, I don't remember any of the drive there which is frightening because I could easily have taken out a pedestrian or two and just driven on like a robot behind the wheel. All the while there was a growing sense of foreboding that I was making a huge mistake leaving Mia. A voice in my head was screaming that I should have stayed no matter how many times she'd told me to leave.

And calm as fuck, too. She hadn't yelled or cried or anything that I would have understood after last night. She'd been cool as a cucumber ordering me out of her house while I'd been like a deer in headlights.

Stunned. It was the only description that fit at the moment. Like most men, I didn't spend an inordinate amount of time pondering my feelings. I knew when I was happy or sad or pissed off. Those were easy. This…this was far more complicated and I struggled to put names to all of the emotions swirling inside of me.

I definitely felt physically sick, the cloying sweetness of the cinnamon roll making me want to wretch out of the car window.

I also had a vague sense of panic that my whole life had changed and I couldn't stop it. Like a runaway train, I could only hold on for dear life and hope it didn't collide with a mountain or an even bigger train.

Luke's door swung open and Rachel stood there, her critical gaze taking me in from head to toe.

"Jesus, you look terrible. You better come in. Luke! Your brother is here and you better break out the whiskey."

I handed her the box with the cinnamon roll in it. "Please get rid of this for me."

Her brows went up but she accepted the box, stepping back so I could enter their home. Luke came out from the kitchen, drying his hands on a towel. He was dressed almost identically to Rachel, jeans and a sweatshirt. They were a cute couple and it was strange that it was the first time I was really noticing it.

A couple. Fuck. I didn't even want to think about that.

"Brother, you look like you just killed a man and ran from the scene of the crime. Do I need to hide you in our basement or get you a fake ID?"

Rachel's gaze bounced back and forth between me and her husband. "I'm going to make a pot of coffee to go with that whiskey."

Luke shook his head. "He doesn't look like he needs alcohol, sweetheart. That would only make it worse. But coffee is a good idea. Black and strong."

"I'm not hungover."

Luke tossed the towel over his shoulder and then placed a guiding hand on my back, leading me into the living room. "That's good news. You do, however, look like death warmed over. What's going on?"

"Mia kicked me out of her house."

I could barely get the words out, let alone believe that it had actually happened. My life was spinning out of control all because she thought she needed to get control of hers. What in the hell was going on?

"She has feelings for me."

I didn't realize at first that I'd said it out loud but the sharp intake of breath from both Luke and Rachel told me that I'd stated it loud and clear. Rachel slapped down a water bottle on the coffee table, her lips pressed together tightly.

"Here's some water while the coffee's brewing."

Looking like she had a whole lot more to say, she stood there with her arms crossed over her chest and her toe tapping against the maple flooring.

"Thanks."

There was silence after I thanked her and I didn't know what else to say. Hell, I wasn't even sure what I was feeling except shocked.

"Maybe," Luke began, settling onto the couch with me. "Maybe you should start from the beginning. We saw that you left with Mia last night and we heard that you punched out her date. Rachel and I thought that was a positive move forward for you two."

"We thought you were finally removing your head from your ass," Rachel said, bitterness lacing her tone. "But if you were smartening up you wouldn't be here right now. You did something stupid, didn't you?"

Offended, I took a swig of the water. "I don't have anything up my ass, thank you very much. And I don't know what you mean…a positive move forward?"

"You and Mia," Luke said, his brows pinched together. "We've all been waiting for you two to get together."

Me and Mia?

"What do you mean *all*? Who are all of you?"

"Everyone," Luke shrugged. "Mom and Dad, me and Rachel. Your assistant. The accountant. The waitress at the barbecue place. Everyone. It's obvious how you feel about her."

"She's my friend."

A friend I had fucked last night. It was amazing. In most places on the planet, friends didn't do that to each other, though.

Laughing, my brother wagged his finger under my nose. "She's more than your friend. You punched her boyfriend last night, bro."

"He was being a jerk."

I didn't like that he had his hands on her. They weren't supposed to be there.

"So you punched him? When was the last time you hit someone?" Luke was still laughing as if this entire situation was so fucking funny. "You can't even remember, can you? You hit a guy because you were jealous as hell. Why don't you just admit it?"

"Because it's not true," I protested but the feeling I was getting in the pit of my stomach was telling me that my brother had a point. I didn't go around punching people. Even the ones that desperately deserved it. "I wasn't jealous."

Rachel hadn't said much the past few minutes so I thought I

was in the clear there but she walked up next to me and slapped me on the back of the head. Not super hard but enough to get my attention.

My hand reflexively went to the spot she'd hit. "Ouch! Shit, what was that for?"

"For being stupid," she said calmly, perching on the arm of a chair. "And for probably hurting Mia today. I don't know all of the details but I have a bad feeling that you've broken that poor girl's heart and she hasn't done anything to deserve that."

"She said she deserved better," I muttered, still stinging from Mia's words and Rachel's slap.

"She does," my sister-in-law agreed far too happily. "She deserves a man that isn't as dumb as a box of rocks."

My arm dropped to my side. "Will you stop calling me stupid?"

"No," she shot back. "You can't see what's been in front of your face for years. We've all known. Mia's been in love with you. We could all see it. Now I will give you that it's not obvious. She's played it super cool but after awhile we all figured it out. But we've all seen that you love her too, Josh, and we've waited for you to figure it out. Mia waited too but I guess she got tired of it. I don't blame her, she has to be exhausted and wondering if you're worth it. Spoiler alert, I'm not sure you are."

All of this was news to me. People had an opinion about me and Mia? About our feelings for one another? They needed a fucking hobby and to keep their nose in their own business.

"What makes you think I'm in love with her?"

This time it was Rachel laughing at me.

"What makes you think you're not?"

"Because I would know."

"How many women have you dated and discarded?" Rachel scoffed. "There's always been something not quite right with them or you. Or the timing was bad. Or they wanted three kids and you only wanted two. Maybe you didn't like their laugh or the books they read. All it adds up to is that you've been making excuses for years."

I could feel the heat of anger on the back of my neck, crawling down my spine. "I just haven't met the right woman."

Luke placed his hand on my shoulder when I would have jumped to my feet, pushing me back down into the couch cushions. "Or maybe you've already found her and you're scared shitless of commitment. Because then it would be real and not a game that you control."

"I don't need control."

Even as the words rolled off of my tongue I knew it was a lie. I loved having control. It was one of the main reasons that I worked for myself and not for someone else.

"Fine. You don't need control," Luke said. "And you don't need Mia because you're not in love with her. Looks like you don't have any problems. Your life is perfect."

Fuck. What had I done? My life wasn't perfect and I did need Mia. The question was in what capacity did I want her in my life? Could my brother and sister-in-law be right? And my parents? And the waitress at the barbecue joint?

Was I in love with Mia?

Is this what it felt like, a terrible ripping out of my heart? I already missed her and I hadn't even been gone from her home for thirty minutes. I couldn't picture a future without her smiling face in it. I'd crawl over hot coals butt naked so that she wouldn't feel a moment's pain in her life.

"Luke, I think I'm going to need that whiskey now."

CHAPTER TWENTY-FOUR

Mia

BRUNCH WITH THE girls. I sat at the head of the table and finished my story, waiting for their applause and adulation. I'd done it. I was officially moving on from Josh.

Shelby was the first to speak. "Have you lost your mind? You kicked him out of your house? That's not in the book."

Emmy rolled her eyes. "Then it should be. Good for you, hon. I'm so proud of you. Don't let a man, any man, make you feel any less than your best. He'd be lucky to have you."

I nodded in agreement. "I know, right? But I could tell he was all wishy-washy about it."

"He who hesitates is lost," Ashlyn quoted. "I was rooting for you two so I'm kind of sad. I think you would have made a nice couple."

I did too but Josh had other ideas.

"He actually looked scared," I said, thinking back to that moment when I'd put him on the spot. "What is he so terrified of? It can't be me."

"Commitment," Shelby replied, shaking her head. "He's afraid of commitment."

"Why?" Ashlyn asked. "What makes men so afraid to fall in

love and settle down?"

"They're not really programmed for it," my sister answered, tapping her chin in thought. "From childhood they're told to be strong and silent. Don't cry. Don't show emotion. Then when they meet a woman they're supposed to be all loving and warm. Plus, there's the whole biological thing about spreading their seed. They're not even aware of that one. It's just in their DNA. I don't know Josh's specific reasons but he didn't get to be in his mid-thirties and single by accident. Women chase him all of the time, so he had to have developed some serious barriers to intimacy."

A barrier to intimacy. Was that what all this was? A wall between Josh and emotions? Was I being lazy not trying to knock it down or climb over it?

No.

Women smarter, more successful, and more beautiful than me had tried and failed. The odds of me being the person who finally did it was incredibly small.

Reaching for my purse on the floor, I pulled out the list I'd made earlier that was tucked in a side pocket. "So after Josh left I started making a list of all of the things I want to do in my life, preferably in the next five years."

"That's wonderful," Emmy said approvingly. "I love lists. They're so useful."

We all knew Emmy loved lists. Spreading their seed might be in the male DNA but organization was in Emmy's.

"Let's hear it," Ashlyn urged. "What do you want to do?"

Sneaking a look at my sister, I cleared my throat and began. "The first thing is to find the love of my life."

"That's a good one," Shelby said with a smile. "Love is the best."

That hadn't been my experience but I let that remark slide because my sister was in love and engaged.

I continued. "Please note that I said find the love of my life. Not get married. Not have a family. At this point, I'm happy just to find him. I don't need the other stuff."

Emmy and Ashlyn were nodding but as I'd predicted Shelby was frowning. She was all about marriage and weddings, especially while deep in planning her own. If I'd been seriously dating anyone, I bet she'd be dropping hints to him about proposing so we could have a double wedding.

As if she'd share the spotlight with me on her wedding day. Not even a remote possibility. Shelby loved the idea of being a bride.

Giving her the side-eye, I raised my brows in question. "Any comments?"

"None."

Shelby was as smart as she was successful.

"Number two is that I want to live abroad for a year or two. I'm not sure if it's possible but I'd like to work somewhere in Europe. There's a teacher exchange program at my school and if I sign up now I could be assigned for next fall."

"You can't do that." Shelby's voice had risen and the heads of several diners whipped around to see what was going on. Taking a deep breath, she lowered her voice. "I mean...you can't do that."

Ashlyn frowned. "Why can't she do that? I think it sounds amazing. I'd do it if I could."

Shelby threw up her hands. "I'm getting married in September."

Resting her chin on her hand, Emmy sighed. "I warned you about this. Don't go all monster-bride on us. This isn't about you. It's about Mia. Try again."

My sister, for once, appeared to be speechless. "It's just– well– I'll be newly married and I'll want my sister around."

Emmy's eyes narrowed and she shook her head. "Sounds self-involved and selfish. We get it. You're a bride. I see them almost every day, remember? But you don't get to claim the whole year for yourself. You get one day. One. Day. We don't all just orbit around you."

"I don't think you revolve around me," Shelby protested, her cheeks turning red.

"Are you sure?" Emmy challenged. "Because you just said you didn't want your sister to take a year out and travel because you're getting married. You're a shrink. What do you think that means?"

"I think it means I'm selfish," Shelby muttered under her breath. "What is happening to me? I see white satin dresses and I lose all reason."

"It's bridal fever." Emmy nodded knowingly. "I see it all the time. Perfectly normal people walk into my office and by the time the wedding rolls around they're crazed. I'm shocked that the grooms actually go through with the ceremony. Luckily most brides go back to normal but some never recover. They miss being the center of attention and they resent that they're not treated like a princess every day after their wedding."

"When did this happen?" I marveled. "Is this a modern problem or have brides been like this through history?"

"I blame reality television," Ashlyn stated firmly. "And social media."

"Everyone blames reality television and social media," Shelby replied as the waitress brought our meals. "But that's too easy an answer. We have to look at society as a whole and wonder why we even need to have a special day. I want to understand why I need to have a day where I'm the center of attention. Have I always been like that?"

"Yes," I answered, shoving a fry in my mouth. "Mom and Dad like you best. You're their perfect little princess so it would only make sense that you would want that to continue."

"Ouch," Shelby exclaimed. "That's harsh. Bitter, party of one."

"I'm not bitter. I'm just telling it like it is."

Emmy and Ashlyn had wisely shut up.

"Mom and Dad do not like me best."

"Yes, they do."

"No, they don't."

Did she really want to do this? Because I could do this all day long.

"For heaven's sakes," Emmy said with a yawn. "We do this almost every few months. Your parents love both of you but even I have to admit that your mother brags about Shelby way too much. She's instilled a great sense of self-esteem…in one of her children."

My sister shook a finger at Emmy. "Don't you blame my mother for this."

"Interesting," Emmy smirked. "A shrink that doesn't want to

blame mommy. That must be a first."

"That's so cliché," Shelby replied. "And they love Mia just as much as me. Maybe more."

It was my turn to roll my eyes. "More? Really? What evidence do you have for that statement?"

Groaning, Ashlyn held up her hands in surrender. "Okay, let's not. As much as Emmy and I love these little family debates, they're getting old. No one wins them so they've been rendered moot. Next subject. Mia, Josh is sure to keep trying so what are you going to do when he calls?"

"Not answer. Ignore his calls and texts. He'll eventually give up."

"You didn't learn anything from the book." Shelby sighed and wiped her mouth with her napkin. "Remember what I said about men wanting to compete and strive? The more you ignore Josh the more attractive you're going to become. He'll just ramp up the campaign."

What campaign? There was no campaign here.

"He won't because I asked him straight out if he wanted to try and he didn't."

Emmy leaned forward in her chair, her gaze darting left and right, clearly not wanting to be overheard. "Was it...you know...good?"

Ah, the memories.

"Yes. Most definitely yes."

"If you can say that, then it was twenty times better for him," Emmy declared. "He'll be back, and you'll need to be ready."

"He won't be back."

After telling him the truth about my feelings, I was sure I'd never see or hear from Josh again.

That chapter of my life was closed and finished.

★ ★ ★

I ENDED UP back at my place after I left Luke and Rachel. They'd given me a hell of a lot to think about and I'd had a hard to concentrating on the road when my head was filled with images of Mia through the years. My other girlfriends, too.

Fuck, I'd compared every one of those women to Mia and they'd all come up short somehow. I simply hadn't realized I was doing it until now. Too late. When did I get so scared of love and commitment?

Dad had said that women came too easily to me and I didn't appreciate what I had. He'd also said that I was so busy working on what I wanted to be, I hadn't worked on who I wanted to be.

I wanted to be a good man. I wanted to be the kind of husband and father my dad was.

Okay, but he said it wasn't that easy. What else did I want?

I wanted to be a man that people respected because he did the right thing even when it was difficult.

I wanted to be the kind of person that others could turn to when they had troubles.

I wanted to have a reputation as an honest, hardworking man who cared about the people in his life.

I wanted to be a man that treated women well because they deserved it.

I deserve better. That's what Mia had said. I hadn't been treating her with respect and she'd – rightly – kicked me to the curb. Fucking a woman in the front seat of my car and then dropping her off at her house and leaving was not respect. That was the opposite if I was being completely honest. Mia had to be feeling vulnerable and unsure after we'd been so intimate but I'd been so freaked out I'd practically left tire marks in her driveway getting out of there so fast. I'd thought I was being so brave showing up there the next morning but that had been the coward's path.

The proof it wasn't the right thing to do? I sure as shit wouldn't want to tell my father what I'd done. And my mom? She'd be so upset, especially as she really cares about Mia.

I was a shit with women. They'd all deserved better, although I could mitigate some of the damage by saying that I'd warned them all ahead of time. But the minute any of them looked like they might be getting attached...I was gone.

I had probably become that warning tale that women would tell their friends about. Don't date a guy like him. He's trouble.

Dad was right. It was time to grow up and be the person I wanted to be. I had to do more than just think about it. Words were nice, but actions had meaning.

And Mia? Where did that leave us? Right now there was no *us* but I wanted there to be. I'd been so busy running from love and commitment I hadn't noticed that it was sitting right next to me or eating Sunday dinner next door.

Mia was the one. My one.

Failure to win her love was not an option.

CHAPTER TWENTY-FIVE

Mia

SHELBY POINTED TO a storefront a few doors down the street. "That's the bakery that's going to do the cake. They have a great reputation and all they do is wedding cakes."

I was going to taste wedding cakes with my sister today because Brad had some business thing in Boston this weekend and he didn't have much of a sweet tooth, anyway. I, on the other hand, couldn't wait to try all the cakes, fillings, and icings. I'd triple-checked with Shelby that we would be allowed to taste every flavor if we wanted to. I wanted to. After the week I'd had, I wanted as much sugar and liquor as I could get.

As my friends had predicted, Josh hadn't gone quietly away. I'd been bombarded with texts, emails, phone calls, and even flowers all week. By Friday my nerves were shot and my backbone felt more like jelly. I didn't like my resistance wavering one bit but Josh had a way of slipping under my defenses when I wasn't paying any attention. I'd need to be vigilant at all times going forward until he got the message that I wasn't going to cave.

No one tells you that being strong is exhausting.

"I think you should do a chocolate cake. That's unusual."

From the look Shelby gave me I might as well have said that I wanted to strip and run naked up and down the block. My uber-traditional sister was officially scandalized.

"Chocolate is for the groom's cake," she said as we entered the adorable shop. It was all bright and happy with pink and yellow walls decorated with huge photos of the most gorgeous cakes I'd ever seen. The whole place smelled like sugary heaven and I couldn't stop myself from taking a deep breath of the aroma. I could happily die right here, my face smeared in frosting and crumbs all over my shirt.

"No one will be able to tell what flavor the cake is because it will be covered in frosting," I pointed out. "Don't pick a flavor because you think it's what you're supposed to have. Pick it because it tastes out of this world."

"Maybe," Shelby conceded. "I do like chocolate."

It was a family trait, along with red hair and green eyes.

A smiling woman wearing an apron came out from the back room to greet us. "Hello, you must be the Kellys. I'm Janelle, the owner of Wishful Cakes. Which one of you is the bride?"

"This one," I said, pointing to Shelby. "Shelby. I'm her sister Mia."

"Welcome Shelby and Mia," the woman said, handing each of us a thick brochure and leading us to a table. "We'll get your tasting started. Are there any allergies we need to know about?"

"Shellfish."

Shelby must have been more nervous than I thought to have blurted out that she was allergic to crustaceans. Other than renting the venue, this was the first major decision Shelby had made about the wedding and she was doing it without Brad.

"I don't think they're going to make you a crab cake, sis," I whispered, elbowing her slightly. "Why don't we sit down?"

With pink cheeks Shelby sat down, murmuring her apologies to Janelle. "I'm sorry about that. Habit, I guess. No, we don't have any allergies to worry about but just in case I'd like to avoid peanuts because that's a common issue."

"That's not a problem. Let me go get your first tray."

Sitting across from Shelby, I draped my jacket and purse over the back of the chair, careful not to disturb the couple sitting next to us at another table. The man looked around my age but the bride looked much younger, maybe her early twenties. They appeared to be having a wonderful time tasting their cakes though, laughing and joking.

While we waited for Janelle to come back, I paged through the colorful brochure. The list of flavors was impressive and they could also make gluten-free or dairy-free cakes.

"They have a chocolate chip cake," I said, practically bouncing up and down in my chair. "And salted caramel. You have to get the salted caramel."

I might never fall in love and get married but I now wanted my very own wedding cake. It didn't have to be anything fancy. Just one – or two – layers. No bride and groom topper. Maybe just a lonely woman and all her cats. Did they have toppers like that? Maybe they could do a custom order.

"We're going to have four tiers, I think, so we'll need four flavors. I want the top tier to be something Brad will like since we'll eat that on our first anniversary."

I loved cake but frozen-for-a-year cake didn't sound so good, even to me.

"I've heard some couples just have a re-creation of the top tier done so they don't have to eat old, dried out cake."

"That's a fabulous idea. We'll do that."

"And you might as well get whatever you want because Brad doesn't like sweets and especially chocolate."

I liked Brad. He was a good guy. But the fact that he didn't like chocolate always made me give him the side eye. He wasn't even allergic to it. He just didn't like it.

Janelle had brought out a huge tray of small cake slices alongside little cups of filling and icing, all carefully labeled. There were paper plates and plastic cutlery on the tray as well.

"I'll leave you both to work through these. There are two other trays also. I encourage you to mix and match as much as possible. If you need more of a flavor just let us know. Once you choose your flavors, then you can look through the style books and choose a cake. Unless you already have something in mind, of course."

Janelle left a stack of three binders on the corner of the table and Shelby immediately abandoned the baked bounty in front of her to leaf through the photos of fancy cakes.

"You do that after you pick a flavor," I said, stuffing a forkful of lemon cake and filling in my mouth. "Oh my God, this is so good. You have to try this one."

My sister's gaze darted around the room and then she leaned forward so that no one else would over hear. "Don't judge me. What if I told you that I don't really care which flavor we get as long as it's delicious?"

"Okay... Then why are we here? You could have ordered a cake over the phone."

I could be doing laundry right now. Or napping.

Fingers tapping on the open binder, Shelby gave me a sheep-ish look. "I just want it to be like the cake in my head."

Others might judge my sister, but I wouldn't. She was all caught up in this bride stuff. I'm not sure how it happened but she was. Normally she was far too practical to care about whether the icing was buttercream or fondant but she'd fallen down the rabbit hole and I didn't have a clue how to bring her back to sanity.

"Shelby," I said gently. "Do you think perhaps you've gone a little too far here? That maybe all of this engagement and wedding stuff has started to eat away at your brain cells until you're making stupid decisions? I'm your sister and I want to help."

"I'm not that bad," Shelby protested but I could tell she was taking in my words and thinking about them. "Am I?"

"Not yet. You have time to save yourself. Think about it… You actually said – out loud – that you don't care how the cake tastes. I don't even know who you are when you say things like that. Next thing you know you're going to start talking about lace or satin or roses or tulips and you won't be able to tell me what day it is unless it's in relation to the date of the wedding."

"I just want everything to be perfect."

Ah, there we have it. I'd had an inkling and she'd finally admitted it. Perfection. If I'd just said that she would have lectured me about unattainable goals, but she'd said it so it was fine.

Excuse me while I vomit.

"No such thing. But I have good news for you." Shelby

crossed her arms and sat back in her chair, waiting for my happy news. "If the cake doesn't show up or the band or the flowers, you'll still be married to Brad. That's the whole point of this. It's not just to get to wear a dress and have your picture taken, right?"

Burying her face in her hands, Shelby shook her head. "It's just so stressful. Brad's family is so judgmental and I'm not even sure they like me. I want to show them…"

"How perfect you are," I finished for her. "No one is perfect, Shel. Not even you."

"I know that. No one knows that more than I do. But his family… I just want to show them that I'm good enough for their baby boy."

"You never told me they were giving you grief."

When she finally looked up, her eyes were bright with un-shed tears and her lips quivered. "They didn't until the engagement. I guess I was fine when we were only dating but now that I'm going to be Mrs. Brad Hollingsworth the Third they're looking at me much more closely. And finding me lacking."

Now that just pissed me off. The Hollingsworth family sounded like real snots.

"You're a wonderful person and Brad is lucky to have you."

"You have to say that. You're my sister."

"No, I don't have to say that, and he is lucky. Which he must know because he proposed. Now do you really not care how the cake tastes because I'm having trouble wrapping my mind around that."

Sniffling, Shelby reached for the chocolate chip cake. "I'm

actually dying to try this one with the white chocolate filling."

"And the lemon." I pushed the plate closer to her. "You have to try the lemon."

One hour, two dozen flavor combinations, and a major sugar rush later we were both giggling our heads off. So far Shelby had chosen chocolate chip, lemon, and salted caramel. She was leaning toward a nice sedate vanilla for the final tier paired with a dark chocolate filling.

"I think that sounds amazing. Go for it."

"I thought you'd want me to pick something more exotic."

"Honestly if I eat one more piece of cake I'm going to explode."

I was actually feeling a little queasy. Perhaps ordering myself a wedding cake of my own wasn't the best idea I'd ever had. I'd table it and decide later.

Shelby reached for the binders again. "Now we can decide on a style."

Can a person get heartburn from too much buttercream and ganache? There didn't appear any place to burp in private.

"I'm going to get us a couple of waters," I said as my sister blissfully paged through the photos. There was a water cooler in the corner of the store. "I'll be right back."

Something without sugar was needed right away.

"That sounds good," she said without looking up. "I'll just wait here."

She was gone. In wedding-land. The best thing I could do is let her enjoy the ride. I quickly filled two large paper cups with water and turned to head back to the table when I had to stop short. The man from the couple next to us was standing right behind me quietly waiting his turn.

"Oops! I didn't get any water on you, did I?"

A few drops had sloshed on my wrist but it wasn't a big deal. It was only water but some people were weird about things like that.

He wasn't one of them, thankfully.

He laughed and shook his head and that's when I received my first good look at him. Cute. Very cute. Almost black hair. Dimples. Twinkling blue eyes. Black frame glasses. He reminded me of Clark Kent.

Then I remembered that he was here at a bakery that only sold wedding cakes and it wasn't because his doctor had told him he wasn't getting enough sugar and flour in his diet.

"I'm fine," he assured me again, his gaze wandering to Shelby and then back at me. "Completely dry. So...are you the bride?"

After the week I'd had, the question caught me funny. If he only knew how messed up my love life was right now.

"No, I'm the maid of honor. My sister is the bride."

"Congratulations to your sister. It's sweet of you to help her out with this. Where's the groom?"

"Business trip. Also, he doesn't really like sweets or chocolate."

Shaking his head, he laughed. "I love chocolate so I was happy to come. I'm here helping my sister as well. Her fiancé is in the military and is currently overseas. My name's Gib, by the way."

So he wasn't a prospective groom. Just a really sweet guy helping his sister.

"That's really nice of you. Gib. Not every brother would do something like that."

Was that his actual name or was it short for something?

"Sara is the youngest in our family and the only girl. Now that her fiancé is overseas we're trying help out with the wedding. I volunteered for cake duty. One of my other brothers has volunteered to meet with caterers. Another for flowers and so on." His smile fell for a moment. "Our mom died a few years ago so she can't be here to help my sister."

I was almost in tears listening to the story. It was the sweetest thing I'd heard in a long time.

"That is so lovely of you. I'm sure your sister appreciates it. Does she have any female friends to help as well?"

It was a personal question but I had a lousy edit filter on my mouth most of the time.

"Sort of. Her maid of honor lives several hours away so she can't be here to help with the day to day wedding plans." He scraped his fingers through his hair and frowned. "I'm sorry I'm monopolizing your time. I'm sure you don't want to hear about this. You have better things to do."

Not really. Shelby was poring over the binders along with Janelle. Whatever design was in my sister's head would need to come out and I wouldn't be any help with that.

"You're fine," I assured him. I didn't feel all that nauseous anymore. "It's a nice story and I could use one. I've kind of had a crappy week and your story has restored my faith in humanity. Thank you."

"I'm sorry you've had a bad week." He glanced over his shoulder where his sister and mine were now comparing cakes. "I don't suppose you might want to get a coffee when we're all done here? There's a nice coffee shop around the corner. I can assure you I'm a nice guy and completely harmless."

Had Gib been flirting with me? I was so effin' clueless some-times.

A nice man. Good-looking. A simple cup of coffee. This was a no brainer. To move on from Josh meant going out with other men. This was my chance and a sign from the universe.

"I guess one cup of coffee couldn't hurt."

CHAPTER TWENTY-SIX

Josh

"I DON'T NEED lunch," I growled to Luke as he pushed open the door of the local barbecue restaurant located near the office. "What I need is a drink."

I'd had the worst fucking week of my life. I'd lost count of the number of texts, messages, and emails I'd sent to Mia. I'd even sent flowers and a teddy bear to her work but she was still ignoring me. What did a guy have to do to say he was sorry? I'd messed up and I'd admitted it. Why wasn't she responding?

"It's eleven-forty-five on a Saturday morning. Do you really think you should be drinking this early?"

I did. Wholeheartedly.

"In some cultures they drink all day."

"Then go live there. In the meantime, we're in a small college town in the Midwest. We've got bars on every corner but even we don't drink this early. Wait a few hours and if you still want to drown your sorrows, I'll buy."

The aroma of spices and smoked meat teased my nostrils and reminded me that I'd barely eaten all week, either. My stomach growled loudly, contradicting my claim that all I needed was a shot of booze. It wouldn't hurt to put a good meal into my gut before I drank enough to forget my problems.

"I'll take you up on that," I promised, stepping back when one of the waitresses walked up to seat us. Was she the one that thought I was in love with Mia?

Luke held up two fingers. "Just two for lunch."

We followed her to a table in the corner right next to a window overlooking the busy street. The downtown area was always bustling on the weekends. She set our menus in front of us, took our drink orders, and disappeared into the kitchen.

Without glancing at the menu, I knew what I wanted. "I'll get my usual."

The pulled pork sandwich and steak fries. Not good for my health but great for the taste buds.

"I think I'm going to get the brisk—"

My brother's voice broke off and his eyes widened. I followed his gaze to a table to our left...where Mia sat drinking coffee.

With another man.

Son of a fucking bitch. I hadn't seen her in a week and she was already dating another guy. She'd been serious when she'd said she was moving on. Shit.

I didn't even have the four-lettered vocabulary to express my emotions, supposing that I could even identify them. I was angry. Hurt. Disappointed. What was that other feeling, though? That crushing sensation located around my rib cage? It was new and highly unwelcome.

It might be heartbreak.

A state I'd avoided quite successfully for many years but was now feeling it more acutely than a butcher's knife right in the chest.

"Just stay cool. He's probably just a friend."

The warning tone in Luke's voice didn't help a bit. All I could see through the red tide of anger and betrayal was Mia sitting across from another man. And she was clearly enjoying herself. I'd been fucking miserable for days and here she was laughing and smiling as if all was sunny and bright in her world.

What in the hell had just happened to me? I was officially a pathetic loser, sitting here like a lovesick dork mooning over the popular head cheerleader.

In high school, I had dated the goddamn head cheerleader.

The waitress brought our drinks, temporarily blocking my view of Mia and her new friend and all I could do was sit and stew as she took our order. When she finally left I was able to get another good look at him.

"I've never seen him before. Have you? Do you know him?"

"No, but he looks a little younger than us."

Dragging my gaze away from the happy couple, I gave Luke a withering look. "Are you saying I'm too old for Mia? Because I'm not that much older."

"I'm not saying anything. I'm just making an observation."

Mia stood and walked toward the ladies' room. This was my chance. I hopped up from chair but my brother was just as quick, grabbing my wrist before I could follow her.

"Don't do it. Just don't. It won't end well."

"I have to talk to her."

"She's here with someone else."

"I can see that, asshole. I just need a minute to convince her to talk to me again."

Luke dropped his hand from my arm. "And if you can't?"

"Failure isn't an option."

My brother sighed and sadly shook his head. "Failure is always an option. Mia's upset and rightly so. Maybe you should give her some space."

I would have but I couldn't now. What if she fell for that guy over there?

"I'm only going to talk to her. I won't make a scene."

"This is a bad idea. You're not thinking straight."

That much was true and I couldn't argue his point. But every nerve and cell in my body was screaming at me to follow her, talk to her. Get her back in my life. I wanted to take back all the crap I'd said that day. I did want to try with her. More than anything.

"I'll be back in a minute."

Luke didn't try and stop me again and I strode confidently towards the restrooms in the back of the restaurant. I might look like I had my shit together but inside I was a mess. I needed her to listen to me and give me another chance.

But there was a little voice in the back of my head whispering that I didn't deserve it.

★ ★ ★

Mia

GIB WAS SHORT for Gibson James and he was a nice guy. A contractor by trade, he was the middle child of a big, loud family that included three brothers, one sister, and two yellow labs that belonged to his father but all of the kids spoiled. His mother, adored by her husband and children, had passed away a few years ago after a long battle with breast cancer. It had been especially hard on the youngest child Sara and now that sister was getting married, feeling the loss of her mother a great deal. They'd all vowed to pitch in as much as possible so that Sara would have family to help her.

I was having a great time, too. The coffeehouse had been packed so we'd ended up at the barbecue place that I loved. Turned out, he loved it too, so we'd ordered an appetizer to split and a couple of coffees. He was smart, charming, handsome, and funny. Everything a girl could want in a guy.

And there was absolutely no chemistry between us. None. Zip. Nada.

I wanted to be attracted to him but I wasn't. Not in that *way*.

The waitress refilled our coffees before heading to another table. I poured in a little more cream and sugar, the spoon clanging against the sides of the cup.

"You said back at the bakery that you'd had a bad week. I don't mean to be nosy but what happened?"

I'd already told him a version of my life story after he'd told his. We'd had similar upbringings and our parents didn't even live that far from each other. We'd even gone to high school together, him a year behind me, but I didn't remember him nor did he remember me. After comparing schedules and teachers, I didn't think we'd shared any classes together but he remembered the prom where the theme was Moon Dance and that football game where we'd beaten our crosstown rival and rushed the field.

"Romance issues."

Gib nodded knowingly. "Ah, I see. Love is a bitch some-times."

"It sure is. I'd really rather not talk about it if you don't mind. The fact is I'm all talked out about it. I just need to move on."

"That's not always easy. What's your plan to do that?"

I'd never been the type to play games with a guy and I wasn't going to start today. Shelby's book was far from my mind. "Well, I thought I'd go out on a limb and accept a coffee invitation from a strange man I met in a bakery."

"Hey, I'm not strange," he protested but he was smiling the whole time. "At least not in obvious ways. I suppose it is pretty brave to accept a coffee date with a guy you don't know from Adam. I'm harmless, though."

"You've said that before."

Our gazes locked for a moment and then we both laughed. The entire situation was funny. I was stupid about men most of the time but I could see that he wasn't feeling it either.

"It's okay," I said. "I'm having fun but I don't expect you to ask me out again."

"What makes you think—"

Shaking my head, I waved away his false protests. "You don't have to be polite."

He seemed at a loss for words and then heaved a heavy sigh. "You're a very beautiful and sweet woman, Mia."

"But you're not interested at all."

Raising his brows, he tried to craft an answer that wasn't blunt but then gave up. "I— No. No, I'm not. And I'm sorry because I'm the one that asked you out."

"It's okay." I sipped at the hot coffee, letting it settle my sugar-laden stomach. The garlic toast we'd munched on had helped quite a bit, too. Real food was good. "You're a terrific guy and I should be attracted to you but…"

His blue eyes twinkled. Good, he had healthy self-esteem. "You're not."

"It looks like you'll live. How would we know how we feel if we didn't spend some time with each other? Now we know. We're destined to be just friends."

Sort of like me and Josh. At this rate, I could start my own fraternity with these men that thought of me like a sister.

"A person can always use more friends." He opened the menu that had been left on the table when the waitress was urging us to order more than garlic toast. "How about we order some lunch and as friends we can discuss the work you want done on your kitchen?"

"It's just a small job. No one wants to do it."

I wanted the out of date light fixtures in my kitchen changed out. I wanted new cabinets and countertops too but that wasn't in the budget.

"I don't mind a small job here or there. For a friend."

I was glad I'd accepted his invitation. He was right. We could all use more friends.

"Okay, but I need to run to the ladies' room first. If the waitress comes by can you order me the chicken plate?"

"Will do."

Purse in hand, I headed back to the restrooms to take care of business, lingering at the mirrors to freshen my lipstick and run a brush through my hair. This day had turned out far better than

I'd ever thought it would. Gib was a nice guy. I was already thinking about fixing him up with Emmy or Ashlyn. Would he agree to a blind date? Or maybe I could just invite a bunch of people over to the house for movies and pizza. They could meet casually and he could see who he had chemistry with.

Not wanting to make him wait any longer, I pushed open the door and ran right into the last person I expected to see. Shit. Shit. Shit. My heart stopped in my chest before plummeted to my feet, that sick feeling coming back with a vengeance.

Josh.

And he didn't look happy. At all.

"WE NEED TO talk."

Just as I'd anticipated, Mia tried to brush past me but I moved into her path. This was not my usual way of dealing with issues and I wasn't a fan of these tactics but I was a desperate man on a desperate mission. Losing Mia out of my life wasn't something I could even bear to contemplate.

"I'm done talking."

"Clearly. I see you've already moved on."

Her eyes widened and her lips firmed. I'd made her angry, which was far better than her indifference.

"You have a lot of nerve. I've watched you date every woman in the tri-county area through the years and not once have I ever gotten pissy about it."

No, she hadn't. Mia had always been nice to my girlfriends.

Sadly, I couldn't say that I was feeling too friendly about the guy waiting for her at the table.

"You're a better person than I am," I admitted freely. I was jealous and I hated it. "Who is he?"

"Just a man," she sighed, rubbing at her temple. "It's really none of your business. Now please step out of my way. I need to get back to the table."

I was running out of time. Get to the point.

"I want to try with you."

Her head jerked up but she wasn't smiling with happiness. "What?"

"I said I want to try with you."

"You said you didn't though," she replied, her tone dripping with suspicion. "What changed your mind?"

I'd practiced this conversation a dozen times in my head but it wasn't going the way I thought it would. I decided to deal with her as if she was a cop that had pulled me over. Keep my answers short and to the point.

"I was scared."

"And you aren't now?"

"I still am but you're worth it. I can't lose you, Mia. You're the most important person in my life."

For a moment I saw her waver. I'd had her for a second but then she gathered herself and lifted her chin defiantly. "When did you decide this?"

"I wasn't two blocks down the road after leaving your house when I knew I'd made a mistake driving away."

I just hadn't known why. That had taken a few conversations with my family.

"You didn't turn around."

"No, I didn't. I regret that." I took a deep breath and held it. I had to shove my hands in my jean pockets so she wouldn't see them shake. Everything was on the line here. "I want another chance. I'll do better this time."

"It's too late."

"It can't be. I've hurt you, I know that. But please let me make it up to you. Give us a try."

I'd known Mia since she was a kid and I could practically see the wheels turning in her head. But it wasn't her head I was worried about. Logic would dictate that she give me another chance.

No, it was her heart that was the problem.

I'd been cavalier about caring for her sensitive feelings and now was reaping the consequences of my behavior. Mia had a tender, loving heart and a giving nature. I'd taken advantage of it, not giving back nearly enough. That would all change if she'd just give me the opportunity.

"If I say I'll think about it, will you step aside?"

"I will."

I did as she asked, clearing the path for her. But I couldn't stop myself from asking one more question. "How long do you need to think about it?"

"As long as it takes."

Mia strode away leaving me standing outside the ladies' room like a creepy stalker. I'd won the battle – sort of – but the war wasn't going to be that easy. I'd better gird my loins because I had no doubt she wanted to kick me right in the balls.

CHAPTER TWENTY-SEVEN

Josh

PATIENCE. NOT MY strong suit.

I really wanted to give Mia time. That had been my intention when she'd walked away from me Saturday at the barbecue joint. I was planning on giving her as much time as she needed but as the hours and days had ticked away I had become increasingly restless, unable to sleep, and generally an asshole to be around. By Wednesday at noon, Luke had packed up his briefcase and told me what I could do with the reports I was complaining about. Then he stomped out, telling me he was taking the rest of the day off. I didn't blame him.

Which is how I found myself standing outside Mia's classroom door that afternoon waiting for her last class to dismiss. This wasn't the smartest idea but lately I'd been doing all sorts of questionable things and couldn't seem to stop myself.

The bell rang and the students zipped out of the classroom looking elated that the school day was over. A few gave me the onceover but they were in too big of a hurry to linger long, which meant I was able to slip into her room as soon as the last one left. Mia was stacking folders and shoving them into her gigantic backpack and I was struck immediately by how beautiful she looked.

She'd pulled her fiery red hair into a braid but a few strands had escaped and were caressing her rosy cheeks. Her lipstick had worn off but her lips were still full and inviting. That now familiar feeling in my chest was making itself known again but I was getting used to it. The only problem was now it was accompanied by panic and fear that I might not be able to persuade Mia to give me a second chance.

"Hi."

Pausing, she took a deep breath before giving me her attention. I couldn't tell if she was angry or happy to see me. Maybe neither. "Hi."

"I'm sorry."

"What are you sorry about this time?"

"About not giving you more time. I meant to."

She shoved a few more folders into the backpack. "I don't have much time. I'm the sponsor for the debate team and they meet in ten minutes."

That panicked feeling reared its ugly head again, this time in my gut sending acid up into my throat. At this rate, I was going to be a medical mess within the month.

"Then I'll make this short. I miss you, Mia. You have no idea how much."

She took her time answering but my heart felt lighter when she said, "I miss you, too."

"That's—"

She held up her hand. "But...that's only natural and expected. It doesn't mean that I should start spending time with you again."

In my world it did.

"I know I've fucked this up, but I swear I want to try with you, Mia. Only you." I paused, not sure laying it all on the line was a good idea but then I realized that my dignity wasn't exactly firmly intact. I didn't want to look back on this moment and not have given it my all. "You're the one. I've been comparing every woman to you for years, only I didn't want to admit it. That's why I could never be serious with anyone else. It's been you all this time, and I'm sorry that it took me so long to admit it."

This was her chance to stomp on my heart just as I'd done to her not too long ago. It was like waiting for the executioner's ax to fall. Would she? Could she? Had I killed any love she'd ever had for me with my careless actions?

"That's hard for me to believe."

"I know," I replied, relieved she hadn't thrown my feelings back in my face. "I'm asking for the chance to prove it to you."

"I gave you a chance." Her voice was soft and a little wobbly. Her gaze was turned away but I was sure that if I could see her face I'd see tears shining in those moss green eyes. "That night at the party I gave you a chance and you didn't want it."

"I'm an idiot." I took several steps forward and to my surprise she didn't move away. I was close enough now that I could smell her perfume, a combination of citrus and florals. Light and fresh, just like her. "I'm stupid and I know there's no good reason for you to give me a chance. But I'm asking anyway."

It must have been the right thing to say and do because she finally looked at me, confusion written across her expressive features.

"I don't know what to do," she confessed. "I don't think I

should give you another chance but I can't stop from wanting to."

"You won't regret it," I said urgently, daring to place my hand over hers where it sat on the desk. "You said you deserved better. I can do that. Let me show you how it could be between us."

My heart was beating so fast in my chest I thought it might jump out of my body and dash around the room, but surprisingly it stayed exactly where it was while I waited for the verdict.

And waited. It seemed like the whole world went silent while I stood there.

Finally, her little chin rose up and her eyes narrowed. "I'll give you a chance."

Opening my mouth to speak, she stopped me by shaking her head.

"Don't get too excited here. I'll give you another chance, but in the meantime we won't be exclusive. And we won't be having sex right away either, so you can put that out of your mind. If you're okay with that, then fine…we'll try."

It sounded like half-ass trying to me but beggars couldn't be choosers. Hopefully once she saw how serious I was about this she wouldn't be going out with any other guys. I was planning to make Mia's life so wonderful she wouldn't even bother with another man.

And hopefully we'd be having sex, too. This time in a nice comfortable bed and not in the front seat of my car.

"I agree to your terms. Thank you."

"You may not be thanking me later."

No time like the present to step up and be a decent boyfriend. "Can I help you with all of this? I can carry that for you."

"No, I have it." Mia reached for one more folder and a few of the papers drifted to the tile floor. "Crap. I really need to get going."

Quickly kneeling to retrieve her documents, a single paper caught my eye as I handed it over. "Is this your resume? Are you looking for another job?"

"Maybe. The school has a program where I can switch with a teacher overseas. They come here and I go there. I've been thinking about it for a long time."

What the fuck? I'd never heard her say a single word about it. That panicked feeling was coming back again.

"You've never talked about it with me."

Shrugging, she slid the papers into the backpack and zipped it closed. "It's always been something I've dreamed about."

"And you'd go if you were accepted into the program?"

"Of course."

"Even if we were a couple?"

Uh oh, that chin was getting stubborn again. I'd clearly stepped in it.

"But we're not a couple, Josh. So I can't sit around and not live my life or make plans while you figure out what you want in this world. Frankly, your track record with women isn't all that comforting and it doesn't make me want to cancel all of my plans for the future so I can spend it waiting for you."

Her words were like sharp knives slicing my flesh but I couldn't argue her premise. I did have a lousy history with relationships. Hell, my own family probably wouldn't put money on my making this work with Mia.

"Fair enough. But I hope to change your mind. I've changed."

"I have, too."

I'd noticed and couldn't help but admire her backbone while at the same time cursing it.

"I'm going to show you I've changed because I can see that you don't believe me."

"I'm looking forward to it. Now I really do have to go."

"How about Friday night? Dinner and a movie?" A terrible thought occurred to me. "Unless you already have plans?"

"I guess that would be okay."

Such enthusiasm. Mia was acting like I'd just made her an appointment for a root canal.

"Then it's a date."

It was going to be the best damn date she'd ever been on. I'd make sure of it.

CHAPTER TWENTY-EIGHT

Mia

AFTER WORK I ended up at Shelby's house leafing through bridal magazines. My sister was trying to decide what kind of dress she wanted to wear and I was trying to decide if I'd folded like a cheap tent.

"I gave in."

Shelby shook her head. "No, you stood your ground and Josh came to you. He's agreed to the rules you've laid down. That's not a defeat."

"Is it a win?"

"It's progress. Did he say the L-word?"

"No, but neither have I."

If Josh had I'm not sure I could have survived it. It would have been far too dangerous in a situation that was already fraught with emotion. He'd said he had *feelings* and that was enough to turn my backbone into water.

"Make sure he's the first one to say it. You make him come after you. After all these years of you pining over him, it's the least he can do."

"That wasn't his fault. He didn't know."

Shelby snorted and the magazine almost slid off of her lap.

"He should have. Anyone with half a brain would have figured it out. He's supposed to be some sort of gaming genius but I think he's not very bright."

Speaking of not too bright...

"Have you heard from Brad? When will he be home from his business trip?"

"Friday. I'm meeting him in Chicago for the weekend." She held out the open magazine. "What do you think of this one?"

No. Just...no.

"That dress is huge. You'd be swamped in it. You need to pick something simpler where you won't just be a head and a dress."

"Why am I drawn to dresses that aren't good for me?" she sighed. "All the ones that I should gravitate toward I don't like."

That was my entire history with men. In a nutshell.

"I think this might be a case where you have to try them on. Looking at these pictures are all well and good and it does help you know what interests you but you may love something once you put it on."

Tossing the magazine onto the coffee table, Shelby gave a huge yawn and then a burp. Got to love my sister. She knew when to be polite and when to let her hair down.

"You're probably right. We need to schedule a trip to try on dresses. Now how about we order some dinner and you can tell me all about what you're going to wear on your date this weekend."

Body armor. Preferably head to toe with a double thickness...right over my heart.

★ ★ ★

Mia

I WASN'T THIS nervous on my very first date when I was fifteen. Rich Gabler, a year older, had taken me to a football game and we'd held hands in the bleachers. Then afterward a bunch of us had gone out for pizza, and later I'd kissed him goodnight on my front porch.

Ah, innocence. I miss it sometimes. Back then it never would have occurred to me that this one date could make or break my future.

Since I had no clue where Josh was taking me, I was in the dark as to what to wear. Eventually I decided on a black maxi skirt, a white sweater, and brown boots. It was casual but dressy at the same time. I took extra time with my hair and makeup, cursing myself the entire time for caring what he thought about my looks. Secretly I hoped he was primping in front of a mirror, worried as well. Technically he had more at stake here because he wanted me in his life and I wasn't supposed to care either way.

So when he picked me up I was elated to see the appreciation in his eyes as his gaze raked me from head to toe. Josh looked damn good too, his normally dark curly hair tamed slightly with some product. He was freshly shaved and smelled delicious, his scent curling around me as I sat next to him in the car on the way to the restaurant. He wasn't playing fair tonight.

"You look beautiful."

I certainly did but then so did he.

"Thank you."

I barely knew what to say or do, which wasn't normal at all. The air between us was thick with tension and a whole lot of unspoken angst. This was the scene of the crime so to speak and I couldn't even put my elbow on the armrest without a million hot and sexy images flooding my brain. He had to be remembering it too because where he was sitting was *ground zero*. I was never going to look at a BMW the same way ever again.

A couple of times I thought Josh was going to say something but then he didn't, letting the silence stretch on until I thought I might scream just to hear something…anything. He hadn't even turned on the radio and it was so quiet I was sure I could hear him breathing. I could definitely hear *me* breathing along with my pounding heart. And then there was the matter of the sweat pooling under my hair at the back of my neck.

So far this wasn't the date of my dreams. This was more like a subtle form of torture.

It was when he took a right on Hastings that I finally broke the silence. "Where are we going? Downtown is in the opposite direction."

"We're going to Henry's Cafe. The movie theatre is right next to it."

Henry's Cafe was kind of fancy and I was suddenly glad I'd rejected the pair of jeans I'd been contemplating wearing this evening. Adults went to Henry's Cafe. There were no televisions on the walls and the college kids stayed away because of the prices. They marketed the restaurant as a haven for foodies, which to me meant that the portions were small and the menu filled with dishes that I'd never heard of. The last time I'd been there was on my dad's birthday. I'd had the truffle macaroni and cheese. It didn't taste or resemble the usual orange stuff that I fixed at home and grew up on.

Now I was more nervous than ever because I was going to have act like an adult when I sure didn't feel like one. I didn't feel any older than maybe sixteen right about now and my teenage self was on an improbable date with the most popular guy in school.

Josh parked the car in between the restaurant and the theatre before hurrying around to open my door. I was more than capable of opening my own and he'd never done it before so I wasn't quite sure how to react, allowing him to grab my hand and help me out the vehicle. He didn't let go either as we walked into the restaurant, his hand warm around mine. It felt...nice. It wouldn't hurt anything to hold his hand. It didn't mean that I was giving in or anything. I'd held hands with Rich Gabler after all and he'd only gotten a kiss goodnight at the end of the evening. There had been no sex or declarations of love.

We were seated at a lovely table in a quiet section, far away from the more lively bar but not near the bathrooms or kitchen. I couldn't take the silence between us anymore. At this rate, I wouldn't last through the salad course.

"I didn't realize you liked this restaurant. I've never heard you talk about it."

A really horrible thought occurred to me at that moment. Was this where Josh brought all of his girlfriends? Was this his "official" date restaurant? And the barbecue joint was where he took his "friends" like me?

"I don't come here often. Just special occasions."

Okay, that wasn't so bad. He thought this was a special occasion.

"We came here on Dad's birthday last April."

Smiling, Josh chuckled and took a sip of his ice water. "Now that explains why my mom wanted to come on her birthday in May."

Our parents did talk to each other a lot. Would they be happy about me and Josh?

I placed my menu down on the table, determined to make this evening the best it could be. Walking on eggshells all night wasn't my idea of a good time and I wasn't enjoying being nervous. Josh and I used to like each other's company. Surely we could do that again even with all that was at stake tonight.

Finally, a waitress appeared at the table to take our order. She looked harried and rushed, which didn't go with the vibe of the restaurant at all. She just wanted to take our drink orders but Josh managed to convince her to take our food order as well, which appeared to upset her a little. My request to substitute potatoes for rice didn't go over well, either. Eventually she bustled away and disappeared into the kitchen.

"That was weird," Josh said, his brows pulled down into a frown. "Normally this place has great service."

"Maybe she's having a bad day. She kind of looked like it."

Perhaps she didn't get the memo about it being a special occasion. I was actually kind of glad that the waitress had been acting strangely because it gave Josh and I something to talk about.

"She did seem upset, didn't she? I have a feeling our order is going to be wrong."

I had the same feeling. I was getting the rice and I might as well get used to the idea.

"How was your week? Are you making progress on the storyboard?"

Josh loved to talk about his work so this should do the trick.

"I'm about ready to finalize it. I'd really like you to look it over first though, just to be sure. Maybe you could come by this weekend?"

Assuming that this date didn't explode into a million pieces.

"Sure, I can do that. Are you unsure about any particular issues?"

We chatted about the game but my stomach didn't want small talk. It wanted food and sooner rather than later. Funny how I could be nervous but still starving. My stomach growled loudly right in the middle of Josh discussing some deeply technical problem that I didn't understand in the least. I pressed my hand to my stomach and groaned in embarrassment.

"I'm so sorry. We had an assembly today and I missed lunch."

For a laidback guy, Josh looked super perturbed, which wasn't like him at all. He might be more nervous than he was letting on. "It's been thirty minutes since we ordered and she hasn't even brought out the salads yet. I'm all for giving people a break when they're busy but this is ridiculous."

Flagging down another waitress, Josh asked to speak to the manager. I was uncomfortable with any sort of confrontation in eating establishments because I'd heard way too many stories of food being spit on, but Josh had a point here. It shouldn't take half an hour to get a tossed salad and a few bread rolls.

A rather scared-looking man approached our table, clearing

this throat and wringing his hands together. Whatever he was going to tell us wasn't good news. "Uh yes, I'm so sorry. I'm the manager here and I'm so sorry you've had to wait for your food. I believe you already placed your order?"

"Thirty minutes ago," Josh said, his tone laced with frustration. "We don't even have salads yet and our glasses are empty. We haven't seen our server since she took our order."

The manager nodded and pointed toward the door to the kitchen. "We've had a few issues tonight. I hope you'll accept our most sincere apology. Your meal will be on us. I'll just get Tracy to take your order again."

I didn't understand. We'd already done that. "Again?"

He cleared his throat again and shifted uncomfortably on his feet. "Well, it seems that your server took orders from several tables…and then quit. We had no idea what she'd done until the complaints started coming in."

I'd made a server quit her job. Was it because of the potatoes instead of the rice?

The good news was the ice was officially broken between the two of us. We had plenty to talk about now and ample time to do it.

CHAPTER TWENTY-NINE

Josh

I T WAS SUPPOSED to be the best date ever but the entire evening had gone downhill at sixty miles per hour. Our waitress had quit so it took forever to have dinner and we were starving by the time they fed us. All we could do was wolf down our food like animals after making awkward small talk the entire time. It wasn't supposed to be like this. I was supposed to be dazzling Mia and sweeping her off of her feet.

Because it had taken so long to have dinner, we'd missed our chosen movie and ended up watching another that started later in the evening. It wasn't too bad actually, a murder mystery with an excellent cast. For the first time during the date it felt comfortable between Mia and I. Sitting next to her in the dark I held her hand, my thumb caressing her palm. She didn't pull away and if anything seemed to move a little closer to me. She smelled so amazing it made my head spin, although if I asked her what her perfume was she'd probably just tell me it was body wash or shampoo. It was hard to believe I'd ignored her allure all these years. Clearly, I'd had my head up my ass but I'd pulled it out now.

"It's him," she whispered softly for my ears only. Our faces were inches apart and her warm breath caressed my jaw. "He's the killer, I bet."

"It's the girlfriend," I replied just as quietly, enjoying the closeness. This was more like the relationship that we'd had in the past. "She has stronger motive."

Neither one of us were going to find out who was right. An hour and a half into the film, a blaring buzzer went off and the lights came on. Mia clapped her hands over her ears as people stood and began to file out of the theatre. A voice came over the loud speaker asking us to evacuate because the fire alarm had been tripped.

Son of a bitch.

Wrapping my arm around Mia, I led us both to the nearest exit which put us outside but on the opposite side of the building from our vehicle. Sometime during the movie, a storm had moved in and it was raining cats and dogs out there. There wasn't even a question of waiting it out and hoping that they let us back in to see the end of the movie. By the time we got to the car we were both soaked to the skin, our coats barely any protection from the wind and rain.

I bundled Mia into the passenger seat and then myself behind the wheel, finally shutting the door against the storm. What a crappy night this had been. I'd set out to make it the best date ever and it was a definite contender for worst date in history. Right now she had to be wondering when this night would ever end. I wanted to howl out loud in frustration that the dating gods were working against me.

"I think I have a blanket in the trunk," I remembered, reaching for the door handle. "Let me get it for you."

"No way," she said, grabbing my arm. "You can't go back out there. It's pouring."

"I'm already wet. I can't get any wetter. We're practically ducks."

I turned the heater on even higher when she shivered and tugged her coat around her more tightly. We were probably both going to get pneumonia, a lovely reminder of our romantic date. We could have side by side hospital beds and oxygen tanks.

"Let's just head back to my place and get dried out."

With a sinking heart, I pulled out of the parking lot and headed to Mia's home. I already knew how the evening was going to end. I'd get a polite thank you and then pushed out the front door. Wet, cold, and alone.

The night was a total loss.

★ ★ ★

Mia

WE WERE BOTH chilled to the bone and a sodden mess. We'd have to strip out of our clothes until they dried or risk dying a painful death from pneumonia. The universe was a funny thing. I'd been so sure Josh wouldn't get me out of my panties tonight but here I was anxious to get rid of them.

I'd started the night determined not to let Josh get under my skin, romancing me with flowers and candlelight, but somehow I'd been charmed by his incredible run of bad luck. He was simply adorable when the world was against him.

The question now was what did I want to do about that? A wise woman would send him home right now no matter how cold and wet he was. But the soft-hearted part of me couldn't do it. Instead I was going to have a romantic fire in the fireplace and offer him a hot, soothing beverage. It was a foolish move almost like playing with matches in a fireworks factory.

"If we don't get out of these wet clothes we're both going to catch our death of cold." I flipped the switch for the gas fireplace and then inched toward the bedroom. "You should park yourself right in front of the fire. I'll be right back."

Josh was standing by the front door, seemingly not sure if he should come all the way in. For a confident man he appeared to be hesitant at the moment, unsure of his next move. Certainly nothing had gone to plan tonight... for either of us.

"I should go–"

"You're not going anywhere." I used my best schoolteacher voice and to my surprise he listened. Hmmm...this was an interesting development. I'd have to do this more often. "You're cold and wet. We need to get those clothes dried out. Give me a minute. I'll be back in a jiffy. Seriously, you should get closer to the fireplace."

Whirling on my sock-clad foot I hurried into the bedroom and quickly stripped off my wet clothes, pulling on a soft pair of sweats and a t-shirt. A quick inspection of my bottom dresser drawer revealed what I'd hoped would be there. A pair of ratty denims and paint spattered t-shirt from when Josh had helped me paint the living room right after I moved in. He'd changed here at my place before heading out to meet his brother and a few friends. I'd laundered the clothes but somehow had never given them back.

It might – or might not – have been on purpose. Don't

judge me. It was going to come in handy now.

Sprinting back into the living room, I placed the garments on the coffee table. Josh had done exactly what I'd told him to do and was kneeling on front of the crackling flames of the fireplace, his hands outstretched toward the radiating warmth. "I'll put your clothes in the dryer after you change into these."

Frowning, he inspected the worn garments and then he smiled. A real one and perhaps the first of the evening. "These are mine."

"Of course, they're yours. You left them here after you helped me paint."

It took me a moment for my mind to wrap around what Josh meant. He'd thought I was offering him *another man's* clothing. And he didn't like it one bit from the look on his face.

"I washed them so they're clean."

He'd picked them up but hadn't made a move toward the bathroom. Was he contemplating dropping trou right here and now? We had slept together…but in the dark and in the position we were in I didn't get to see much.

"Yes," he finally said, dragging his gaze from the clothes and back to me. "Thank you. I'll go change."

"Hot chocolate or a glass of wine?"

"Does it sound terrible to say that I could use a glass of wine after the night we've had?"

"I have whiskey, too."

I kept it around for him. Personally, I thought the stuff tasted like old, dirty socks that were on fire. I'd only contemplated drinking it the night of the robbery and never again since then.

"Wine is fine. Thank you."

Josh ducked into my powder room in the hallway and I went into the kitchen to pour two glasses of wine. Now we had the trifecta of seduction....

A toasty fire.

Wine.

Not many clothes.

There was also the bonus fact that I was incredibly attracted to Josh and couldn't put our one time together out of my head. I'd been so sure nothing would happen tonight but I was now in the position that something definitely could happen.

I couldn't say that I was innocent, either. If I'd truly not wanted anything to happen I should have said goodnight at the door. But I hadn't done that. If anything, I'd insisted he come in and take off his clothes. Was I the seducer tonight? Had I unconsciously done all of this so that I could get Josh in bed again?

The entire situation was ridiculous because Josh was a guy. It probably didn't take much to convince him to have sex. Even with me.

All because there was something in the air between us. A tension that wasn't about the date going well or wanting to impress me. It was more primitive than that, more...sexual. As stupid as I was I could feel it. Josh had wanted to leave because he'd felt it, too. We were both thinking about the other night.

What did either one of us intend to do about it?

CHAPTER THIRTY

Josh

I N MY HEAD, I kept repeating *it's just Mia* over and over but the rest of my body wasn't receiving the message. My heart was slamming against my ribs and parts farther south were perking up at just how incredibly adorable she looked in her old sweats. Her hair was still damp from the rain and I wanted to reach out and pluck at a red-gold ringlet, stretching it and then letting it bounce back.

She held out a glass of wine and I could see her hand tremble. Slightly and ever so briefly. But it made me feel better. She was nervous too even if she didn't outwardly display it. I accepted the glass and took a fortifying sip. It had been one crappy night, and I was still a little on edge wondering what was going to happen next.

"This wasn't how the date was supposed to go," I found myself blurting out. "I had it all planned."

Her smile was gentle and she stepped past me to settle on the floor in front of the fireplace.

"I know. But I'm actually kind of glad it all went the way it did. I think I would have been way more nervous if it had all gone the way you planned it."

She was admitting to being nervous. Courageous. I wasn't quite as brave as that. I was supposed to be the kind of guy that knew what to do with a woman. Not that you'd know that by how I'd acted tonight. My father's words echoed in my brain for the millionth time. Women had come far too easily to me.

I had to work now.

"I just wanted our first date to be special."

"It was special but it doesn't always have to be, Josh. I'm happy just hanging around the house or eating barbecue and watching the game."

"You hate sports."

"But I like it when you try and explain it." She patted a large pillow next to her. "Come sit and get warm."

"I think you secretly understand football but pretend not to. No one can be that confused about first downs."

She held up two fingers. "Sure they can. There are two types of first downs. Two, Josh."

"No, just one."

"Two." She counted off on her fingers. "The first is the first down when they get ten yards. The second is the first down out of four downs. Two."

"The second one is just down number one. It's not a first down. See? You do understand it."

She grumbled under her breath about men and not being good at naming things which only served to make me smile. This was the Mia I'd come to know and love. I didn't want her to feel like she had to be or do anything differently. I wanted her just the way she was.

"It's the first of the four downs," she finally said. "You know

I'm right. How's the wine? It's a new one I picked up at the store last week. It's Australian."

I took another sip as if I knew about wine. I didn't know shit. "It's good, although I prefer a dark ale."

We'd run out of conversation again, that tension that had followed us around all night firmly planted between us. I'd begun to think of it as a threesome. Me, Mia, and Tension. That little asshole was really starting to get on my nerves.

I'd also noticed that the atmosphere was really romantic with the two of us sitting in front of the fire and the lights low. I was getting all sorts of ideas but I didn't do a thing about them, instead sitting next to her and saying nothing.

Awkward.

"How about I pop in a movie?"

A movie? Yes, that would be a good idea. I wouldn't be expected to talk and make conversation like a grownup. I could stare at the television and take my time thinking up things to say. Or I could simply talk about the film. A nice, neutral topic.

"That sounds good."

"What are you in the mood for?"

Not romance. Or any love scenes. Or feelings. I didn't want a bunch of messy emotions because I had my own. I needed fiery explosions, gunfights, pulse-pounding suspense danger.

"How about *Jurassic Park*?"

There wasn't anything remotely romantic about dinosaurs.

Josh

I'D CHOSEN THE wrong damn movie. I'd forgotten that Mia hated the part when the velociraptors chased the kids into the kitchen and those scaly bastards sniffed and snuffled their way around, scaring the bejesus out of the woman sitting next to me on the couch. A few minutes ago there had been about six inches between us but now she was cuddled up close and semi-hiding her eyes. Her fingers had a death grip on my arm and I placed it around shoulders to assure her that there were no rogue dinosaurs in her condo. She'd done this many times before when we'd watched this movie but tonight…

It was different.

Or I was different. No quibbling on the details but I was hyper aware of every centimeter of Mia pressing against me. Her unique fragrance. The heat and weight of her body. Living dangerously, I allowed my fingers to rub a silky strand of her hair. The blood was already beginning to drain from my frontal cortex to my cock. Soon I wouldn't be able to make any decent decisions or even do basic math. All reasoning skills were off the table and my caveman needs were firmly in control. The ones that told me to drag her off to my three-bedroom air-conditioned cave and show her who she belonged to. An action that would surely get me kicked in the balls.

She shuddered and cuddled closer. "This part is so scary."

"I won't let any mean dinosaurs get you."

Mia looked up at me, total trust in her expression. It was like a punch in the gut and I could barely breathe. "I know."

The moment was here. Her face was upturned at a perfect angle. I only needed to lean down a few inches and our lips would be touching. I'd been thinking about this all damn night. Hell, who was I kidding? I'd been thinking about this for days. A gentleman would have backed off but I couldn't do that. I was only human and this woman had been driving me crazy to the point where I'd barely slept or ate.

Leaning closer, I hesitated for only a split second, trying to give Mia a chance to back away and say no. Instead her eyes fluttered closed and I pressed my lips against hers, so full and soft.

CHAPTER THIRTY-ONE

Mia

SAYING NO NEVER crossed my mind. I'd been lying to Josh and myself about seeing other men and not sleeping with him. I wanted to make love with him. Only now, I wanted to take my time and savor every moment.

That night in the car I hadn't been able to see or even touch him all that much. He'd been mostly dressed but I'd be a liar if I said that I didn't want to see him gloriously naked, every inch of him exposed for my exploration. I would happily lend him my body as well if he wanted to return the favor.

The kiss changed from tentative to demanding, his hand curling around the back of my head so I couldn't pull away. Not that I would have. I was in this, totally willing and on board with every dirty thing he might want to do. In fact, I had a few on my list too. We could take turns. I wasn't planning on lying back and being a silent partner in the bedroom. When I'd said that I wanted to go after what I wanted in my life, I meant in all facets. Especially sex. Too many times it had been mediocre or unsatisfactory because I'd been too timid to tell the guy what I wanted or needed.

Of course, Josh was practically a mind reader when it came

to lovemaking. I hadn't had to tell him anything that first night but the whole thing could have been simply dumb luck. I couldn't count on that every time.

His lips trailed over my jaw and down the sensitive flesh of my neck. Shivering with arousal, I gripped his shoulders as the world tilted and spun on its axis. So very good. Rough fingertips stroked the exposed flesh of my belly where my sweatshirt had ridden up. These clothes were in the way and I was already impatient, wanting to get closer. As close as we could possibly be. Garments just slowed us down.

"Yes," I whispered as his questing hand slipped down past the waistband of my sweatpants to cup my bottom. There would be no misunderstandings tonight. We both wanted this. "More."

Josh's answer was to kiss me again, harder and slightly more desperate. I slid my hands under his thin t-shirt, loving the way his muscled back shifted under my palms. It was romantic here in the firelight but the thin rug on the floor wasn't the best place to slowly make love. We'd both end up with sore backs and knees tomorrow.

"Let's take this to the bedroom."

NOTHING HAD EVER felt this good in my entire life. We'd shed our clothes, tossing them carelessly aside on the way to Mia's bed and now we were skin to skin, completely bare. The only light in the room was a few candles Mia had quickly lit and they flickered with each turn of the ceiling fan, casting dancing shadows on the walls.

There were no more secrets between us, including whether Mia's freckles continued farther down than her face. She did indeed have them all over her body as if magic dust had been sprinkled on her creamy skin. I pressed kisses to her shoulders, connecting the dots with my tongue just as I had in my fantasies. Her response was even more than I'd hoped for, her torso bowing off of the mattress and her fingers tangling in my hair. She whispered my name a few times as I kissed a damp trail down her torso, determined to hear her scream it as she orgasmed.

"Josh."

Her voice was a mere whisper in the dark silence. I could hear our breaths and gasps, the sound of skin on crisp linen but it was hard to see her expression in the dim light. I had to go on instinct as to whether she was feeling as much pleasure as I was. Just being with her this way was more than I'd hoped for just a week ago. I thought for sure that I'd blown it forever.

Forever. Would I be lucky enough to have this woman that long? I could see us in thirty or forty years sitting on the back porch of a large family home and watching our grandkids playing in the backyard. Our hair would be gray and our bodies not as fit but that glint in her eye would tell me that she still felt the same passion that we had tonight.

Pushing her thighs apart, I let my tongue trace patterns on her inner thigh, watching her writhe and moan as I grew closer to where she needed me the most. I pressed one then two fingers inside of her, crooking them to find her sweet spot that would hopefully send her over the edge while my mouth played with the shiny pearl on the outside. A winning combination that immediately sent her flying into space, calling my name as the climax took control if only for a little while.

Eventually she came back to earth, her fingers carding through my hair and rubbing at the stubble on my cheeks. I loved that Mia was so tactile, wanting to touch me as much as possible. I wanted to do the same with her.

"Wow," she said softly. "That was amazing."

I could feel the heat rushing to my cheeks at her praise. I'd heard it before from other women but this was the only one that truly mattered. The others? Sadly, they'd only been a warmup for the real thing. The one. Although I was damn glad that I wasn't an inexperienced boy that didn't know how to please a woman. I was damn proud that I could make her come so easily.

"You're pretty amazing too." I slid up her body, pressing kisses on the way until we were eye to eye. "You're so responsive."

Her soft hands were running up and down my back now, sending shafts of pleasure straight to my balls and cock. They were demanding their pleasure as well, my lower back already aching from holding back. But we'd rushed it last time. I wanted to make it last more tonight. I'd fantasized so many times about what it would be like with Mia. This might not be our first time, but it felt like it.

Her lips turned up in a smile and my chest tightened as my heart grew too large for my ribcage. I loved this woman so much and she had no idea. How was that possible? And how did I not know before? I was fucking stupid, that was how.

"How could I not be responsive? You know what you're

doing."

"You're good for my ego."

That made her laugh, a sound that was music to my ears. "I don't think your ego needs any help but I guess that's alright. You know, I kind of want to make love to you, too. What do you say? Can we switch places?"

Hell yes. I eagerly rolled onto my back anxious, to feel her hands and mouth on me. In the car we hadn't had much time for foreplay and it was good to have the chance to savor each other a little. Just seeing Mia straddling my hips, her incredible nude curves hovering above me had me harder than solid steel.

So detail oriented, Mia started at my forehead, pressing baby kisses all the way around my face and then down my neck. She nipped at my shoulder where she'd placed a bruise that first night but much softer this time. Her tongue ran over my collarbone and then down between my pecs before taking a side path and running around my nipple. My breath caught in my throat and the blood thickened in my veins as my arousal soared. She'd barely touched me and I was hard and ready to go.

That devilish tongue danced down over my abs, dipping in my belly button on the way down, before taking a long lick from the base of my cock to the tip almost like I was a delicious ice cream cone. Giggling, she did it again and again until I was cursing and gritting my teeth, an explosion imminent if she didn't give me a moment to collect myself. Running my hand up her silky thigh, I gave her bottom cheek a squeeze.

"I wanted to take this slow, honey, but I don't think I can wait anymore. I want you so much."

I barely recognized my own voice, so full of need and desperation. Mia didn't even blink an eye though, so perhaps she felt the same. Reaching into her nightstand, she pulled out a box of condoms. Thank goodness one of us was thinking straight. I didn't have any blood left in my brain to do anything more complicated than fuck us both into paradise.

With shaking fingers, I rolled on the condom before grasping her hips. She anchored her hands on my chest as she lowered herself down slowly, inch by damn inch, her eyes closing and a smile blooming on her face when I was balls deep. So fucking good. Mia was hot, wet, and tight, hugging my cock with a velvet grip. I had to grit my teeth not to come right away like a callow teenager. I wanted Mia to come again before we were done.

Mesmerized, I watched as she rode me, her breasts bouncing with every thrust. Reaching out, I cupped those beauties in my hands, caressing the pebbled nipples with my thumbs. As beautiful as Mia riding me was...and it was goddamn gorgeous...we'd done this before in the car. Now that we had a comfortably soft mattress underneath us I had something else in mind.

Quickly rolling her underneath me, I captured her lips with my own, letting our tongues mimic our bodies. We were both giggling but it turned serious as I snapped my hips forward, my groin stroking her clit as I thrust in. Again and again I did it, watching Mia's expression go from playful to blissed. Her walls were tightening on my cock and I could tell she was close, which was good. I wasn't sure I could hold off my own orgasm much longer.

Covered with sweat and holding on by a thread, I lifted

Mia's leg slightly to get a better angle, speeding up as her nails dug into my back. The crude sound of our damp flesh slapping together was loud, as were our moans and grunts. This wasn't the gentle coupling I'd planned but it was far better and satisfying. Mia was a woman who let me know that she liked what I was doing. It was the sexiest thing I'd ever experienced and I felt about ten feet tall.

"Harder," she panted, her face glowing and her eyes heavy-lidded with desire. "Don't hold back. I want it all."

And I wanted to give it to her but I wouldn't be deterred from my original mission. Her supreme pleasure. Reaching between us, I placed a thumb on her clit and began to make quick circles around the swollen button. That's all it took.

Mia went off like a rocket, her channel clamping down on my cock like a vise and sending me over as well. My climax ripped through me, excruciating in its intensity, and when it was over I fell on top of her completely wrung out and spent. Despite the fact that she could probably barely breathe Mia didn't complain, content to enjoy the closeness. Her fingers glided up and down my spine until I gathered enough energy to roll off of her poor, squashed body.

Tucking her into my side, I let my fingers run through her long hair as fatigue overcame my body and my lids grew heavy. For the first time in a long while I was content. I had Mia by my side and this time I wasn't going anywhere.

We'd wake up together. The first of many mornings to come.

CHAPTER THIRTY-TWO

Mia

AFTER SCHOOL ON Monday, I stopped at Emmy's office and helped reorganize the shelving units. Binders with cake styles on one shelf, binders with dresses on another, and so on. Anything that wasn't bridal went on a different bookshelf altogether. When we were done we were going to dinner with Ashlyn near her retro shop. Ashlyn owned the biggest and best shop of retro items in the entire Midwest. She specialized in hard to find vinyl albums and novelty pieces in their original packaging such as Silly Putty or a Pet Rock.

"It's just that I think I gave in too easily," I said, sliding in a heavy binder on the bottom shelf of a huge bookcase that I prayed was attached to the wall. Otherwise, if it fell I'd be roadkill.

Emmy was standing on a small stepladder loading up the top shelves. "I don't think you did anything wrong. You have feelings for each other and you expressed them in a physical way. Very understandable."

Feelings. Such a wimpy word for all the emotions that I had swirling inside of me.

"Shouldn't I have made him work harder?"

Chuckling, Emmy climbed down the ladder to grab another armful of books. "Did he make you be on top?"

My face went hot at the memories. "No. That's not what I meant. It just seems like I should have done something...different."

"You mean played hard to get?"

"Yes," I admitted. "Although when you say it like that it sounds bad. I don't like the idea of playing games in any relationship, least of all with Josh."

Placing the books on a table, Emmy sat down on the floor with me. "Why don't you cut to the chase and tell me what you're worried about? Did he not call the next day?"

I smiled at the memory. "He didn't have to. He was still there. He brought me breakfast in bed."

"He sounds like a real loser," Emmy taunted with a grin. "A man who cooks for you is so awful. Whatever you do, don't have sex with him. Did he call the next day?"

"He called me on the way home. He called me that night. He called me the next day, and we even got together for barbecue last night."

"Then I'm not sure what your complaint is. He sounds like he's all in."

"How long will it last?"

Giving a voice to my fear was supposed to help but I was still scared to death. It was worse than those velociraptors.

Emmy's smile faded. "I don't know. No one can keep up that sort of intensity forever and I think if you're honest with yourself you wouldn't want him to. You'd feel smothered and stalked. But for now it's nice."

"He's always put his career first. Always."

I didn't want to be the afterthought in Josh's life. I deserved to be a priority. Not the only one, of course. I wasn't delusional. But I needed to know that when the chips were down, he'd be there.

"I know you don't want to hear this but he can't change who he is on a dime. You need to give him some time. He might make some mistakes but it sounds like he wants you in his life and is willing to do what he needs to make that happen."

I wanted to trust and believe but it wasn't easy.

"I want to change the subject to something far more pleasant," I announced. "Saturday night. My place. I'm having a game night. Gib will be there. I want you two to meet."

Emmy gave me a shrewd look. "If he's so great how come you didn't want him?"

"Because of Josh, which you know perfectly well. Gib is a great guy and I think you'd like him. This isn't a fixup. I'm inviting him, you, Ashlyn, Shelby, Brad, and Josh. If you or Ashlyn happen to hit it off with him that would be great. If not, that's okay, too."

"So it's kind of a fixup."

"Think of it as a mixer. You might want to get to know Gib better or you might not. But he's a super nice guy and if nothing else he's my new friend."

"That you met at a cake tasting," Emmy laughed. "Are you sure you don't want him? That would be a great story to tell the grandkids."

So would being in love with Josh all of my life, but happily ever after might simply be out of my grasp.

MIA AND I had been dating – officially – for a week. I'd talked to her every day and we'd been out a few times during the week, although not too late since we both had to work. Things were going well but I could tell I was still on probation. She was waiting for me to fuck up and I was determined not to do anything stupid. Only time would tell if I could manage it.

Right now, I was trying to win the best boyfriend ever medal and lend a hand with the little party Mia had decided to throw. Game night. She loved board games and it went without saying that I did, too. We'd already played a round of Clue and everybody was getting a fresh drink to go with the pizza that had just arrived. After we ate, we were planning to start the grand-daddy of all games, Monopoly. No one wanted to do that on an empty stomach.

Mia joined me in the kitchen where I was making a pitcher of margaritas. The pizza boxes were laid out on the table and the smell of garlic and tomatoes was making my stomach growl.

"I think it's going pretty well, although Gib doesn't seem to have any chemistry with either Ashlyn or Emmy."

I didn't want to like Gibson Davis but dammit, he seemed like a decent guy. When Mia had told me she wanted to have a game night and invite her friends I was thrilled. I was being trotted out as the official boyfriend and that was progress as far as I was concerned.

Then she said that she was inviting her new friend Gib so

that he could meet Emmy and Ashlyn. This wasn't welcome news. She'd assured me that Gib didn't think of her in a romantic way but I was having a hard time believing that. She was so amazing how could he not be smitten? Was he stupid?

Mia had warned me to be nice and I promised I would. It wasn't as difficult as I thought it would be. He didn't hover around her or try and get her alone. He had his own business like I did, so we had that in common. He also liked sports and craft beers so we had topics to talk about. A hell of a lot more than I had in common with Shelby's fiancé Brad. So far he'd spent most of the evening in the spare bedroom talking on his cell phone with someone in Los Angeles. Or Hong Kong. I hadn't really been paying attention so it could have been Kathmandu for all I knew.

"I never knew you were such a matchmaker," I replied, putting the cap back on the tequila bottle. The drinks were set up on the kitchen counter so guests could go smoothly from the food to the beverages. Emmy, party planner extraordinaire, had made sure we efficiently organized. "It's still early in the evening. You never know what might happen."

"That's true. It only took us twenty-five years or so."

Ouch. Mia knew where to stick the knife.

"Hopefully Gib is smarter than I am."

I'd teed it up for her but she didn't take a swipe at it. The old Mia would have but it was kind of sweet that she didn't this time.

"I don't know why Brad even bothered to come," she said softly, moving closer to me so she could keep her voice down. "He makes me crazy sometimes but it doesn't seem to bother

Shelby."

It didn't, which was a testament to her patience and ability to give Brad the space he needed to go after his goals and dreams. That's how I'd always pictured my marriage. Each of us giving the other the space and opportunity to be successful.

It was strange to see it from the other side, though. I didn't have a high opinion of Brad because he wasn't paying any attention or time with Shelby. From the expressions of disdain on the other partygoers I wasn't the only here tonight that felt the same. So what did that say about me when I acted that way? I didn't like to think that Brad and I had anything in common... But we did.

It wasn't a comfortable feeling. I didn't want to be that guy and I sure as shit didn't want to treat Mia that way. She deserved better, a fact she'd shared with me that night she'd ordered me out of her house.

"Shelby has a lot of her own stuff going," I finally answered. "She might be relieved he isn't breathing down her neck about the wedding plans. She can have whatever she wants."

I'd always thought I would be the same type. Not care about the flowers or the cake but I'd found myself actually talking to Shelby about it, interested in the choices she'd made so far. I'd want an outdoor wedding, maybe at the beach. Not that there was a beach anywhere in the plains of Illinois.

Mia shrugged as if she didn't care but her body was tense. She did care. "I just want her to be happy. Sometimes..."

"Yes?" I prompted. "You know you can tell me anything, right?"

"I know. It's just I hate to even say it out loud." She poured herself a margarita and took a sip, grimacing a little. I'd made them strong. "Okay, here it is. Sometimes I think that maybe Shelby marrying Brad is a mistake. He loves her and that's terrific. But...he doesn't...make her the best version of herself. Do you know what I mean? She's not happy and relaxed when he's around. And it's not just the wedding. It's always been this way. She's stiffer and more formal. She's someone else and I'm not sure that I like her as much."

I did know exactly what Mia was talking about. I'd seen it, too.

"In five or ten years, Shelby will probably act the same around Brad. Hell, maybe even worse. She's a certain way with you, your parents, old friends because she's known you all forever. Brad is newer in her life."

That earned me an eyeroll. "They've dated for years. Years, Josh."

Another strange thing about Brad. He'd been in absolutely no hurry to tie the knot with Shelby. He'd blamed getting his career going but he was in his late thirties. If he didn't have his career going yet, he needed to reevaluate his goals.

"I probably don't know what I'm talking about. I don't know shit about relationships, remember? I'm just learning." I paused, holding my breath. Did I dare say it? It was the truth. Why not? "You make me the best version of myself, Mia. I hope I do the same for you."

She'd been about to take a drink but instead she set the glass down, carefully keeping her gaze trained on the countertop. I didn't say anything else, honestly not sure what to do. Had I fucked up? The silence stretched painfully on until I had to force myself to take in oxygen even though my chest was tight and hurting. Right about where my heart was located.

Finally she turned her gaze to me, her usually bright green eyes more gray. There was a storm going on in Mia's head and I was terrified of the outcome. "I want to believe you. More than anything. I'm going to get everyone so they can eat before the pizza gets cold."

Without another word she exited the kitchen, leaving me standing there still processing her words. I'd fucked everything up so badly. Even now Mia didn't have a clue as to how much she meant to me, and I didn't know how to help her see it. The only thing I knew to do was to hang in there. Show her. Actions spoke louder than words.

Would she give me the chance to make her trust me? Had I already lost and just didn't know it?

CHAPTER THIRTY-THREE

Mia

I DIDN'T HAVE anything to complain about. Josh had been terrific in the last week, making sure that I felt important in his life. I had kept him at arm's length however, using the excuse that we both had to be up early in the morning for work. Since Saturday night all we'd done was kiss. Passionate kisses to be sure, and frustrating as hell, but I was still feeling unsure about whether I'd done the right thing by sleeping with him again. So far he was convincing me I had but I still wasn't sure I could trust my own eyes.

Josh appeared to be the very picture of a devoted boyfriend. I simply wasn't sure if eventually he'd get tired or bored and go back to his old ways.

"You're frowning," Ashlyn said when we took a break from the Monopoly game to refresh our drinks and get some dessert. As usual Emmy was killing it and building a real estate empire. I had about fifty bucks of play money and one valuable utility.

Ashlyn had made a chocolate cake that looked delicious and I'd whipped up a cheesecake that I retrieved from the refrigerator. "You should be happy. It looks like it's all working out for you."

"You sound like Emmy."

Ashlyn glanced over her shoulder to where the rest of the guests were huddled around the booze. Josh was playing bartender and mixing drinks. "What about Shelby? What does she say?"

"She seems happy for me." I sighed and slumped against the fridge, keeping my voice down. "I may have not told her about Saturday night."

Brows up, Ashlyn gave a nervous laugh. "And may I ask why not? Never mind, I think I know. That crazy book, right? If it's not in there she doesn't want you doing it."

"I've abandoned the book," I admitted, clutching the cheesecake tightly. "Nothing is going as planned."

"But it's good?"

"So far."

"You're afraid to let yourself be happy."

"That's right. And for good reason. You'd be afraid, too."

Sneaking a glance at Josh, Ashlyn smiled. "He looks pretty taken with you. Maybe you should give him a chance."

To steamroll my heart and flatten it like a pancake. Just like that coyote in the cartoons when an anvil falls on his head.

"That's easier to say than to do."

"You can't make it work like this, with one foot out of the door. You've asked him to commit. It isn't fair not to do it yourself. I know you wanted to keep your options open but now that you've slept with him again things have sort of changed. You're a couple and you're together. Now let's cut that cheesecake. Is that salted caramel sauce on the top?"

"It is," I confirmed but my mind was still back at what my

friend had said. She had an excellent point. I couldn't ask Josh to do something that I wasn't willing to do myself. "Thanks, Ashlyn. I'm going to think about your advice."

"Advice? I didn't give any advice. I simply made an observation. Whether you think I'm correct or not is up to you. Personally, I think I'm freakin' brilliant."

I had to agree. If I wanted Josh to be all in, I had to be too. I had to conquer this annoying as hell fear that he was going to hurt me. I had to offer him a little trust.

★   ★   ★

"YOU GAVE EMMY a run for her money tonight. She's pretty much unbeatable at Monopoly."

At the end of the game it had come down to Josh and Emmy squaring off for world domination. Emmy had ended up the winner but she hadn't had any easy time of it. Josh loved games and he was incredibly competitive to boot. He wasn't going down without a fight.

Despite his stinging loss, he'd stayed behind to help me clean up after everyone else had gone home. Shelby didn't even linger like she usually did. From what I could tell, she and Brad were going to have a nasty argument in the car on the way home and then not speak to one another for a few days. Brad hadn't budged from my spare room most of the night and at first Shelby hadn't minded but eventually she'd tired of everyone asking about her erstwhile fiancé. Brad on the other hand looked like he didn't have a clue as to why she was mad. Knowing my sister – and I did know her well – she was going to spend the next hour or so educating him.

I almost felt a little sorry for Brad.

"That girl is crazy competitive," Josh said, rinsing glasses in my sink. "I think she hates to lose more than she likes to win."

I tapped my chin as if deep in thought. "Hmmm…who does that sound like? Could it be…you? You're one of the most competitive people I've ever met. You're only describing yourself."

He dried his hands on a dishtowel and then reached out to pull me into his arms. Shivering in response to his casual touch, I looped my arms around his neck as we kissed. Softly at first and then more urgently, our emotions finally being let free after being bottled up all week. I lost track of time as our caresses became more intimate, his hand skimming under my sweater to stroke the bare flesh over my ribcage right under my breast while my fingers snaked up into the silky curls at the nape of his neck.

That saying about not being able to stand the heat in the kitchen was absolutely true. The temperature had soared and all I could think about was dragging this gorgeous man back to my bedroom and having my wicked way with him. He must have had the same thought because he reluctantly lifted his head, his breath ragged and labored.

"If we keep this up…"

He didn't have to finish that sentence. We both knew what he was saying. At the beginning of the evening I might have pretended to be more tortured about making the decision but after talking to Ashlyn it was a done deal. I had to be all in too no matter how scary it was.

Just stand on the edge of the cliff and step off. No problem. Whatever you do, don't look down.

I glanced at the dishes piled in the sink and then back at Josh. The leftovers had already been packed away in the refrigerator. "Those will keep until morning. Let's go to bed."

His eyes widened and his mouth fell open slightly. I'd surprised him. Heck, I'd surprised myself. The best way to jump off of a ledge was to just go ahead and do it. I was going to act like Josh following me into my bedroom and spending the night was the most natural thing in the world. As if we'd been doing it forever and were some old couple that could complete each other's sentences.

"Good idea," he finally said, pulling me by the hand out of the kitchen, perhaps afraid I might change my mind. "I should have brought my toothbrush."

"I have an extra. You know…for when you stay over." I took a deep breath and plunged in all the way, my heart in my throat. I'd been assuming that he was all in. What if he wasn't? "You could keep a change of clothes here, too. If you wanted to. I could clear out a drawer or something."

Josh leaned down to kiss me, his hand gently cupping my jaw. When he lifted his head his eyes had turned dark blue. "I'd really like that. And the same for you. I mean, you can leave whatever you want at my place. I'll clear out as much space as you need."

Our gazes locked and a quiver ran up my spine at what I saw. It looked like love. I wasn't the most experienced at spotting it and I wouldn't bet the farm or anything but that's what it looked like to me. Did I dare believe my lying eyes?

"That sounds like a good plan," I said instead of what I really wanted to say. That I loved him still and I hoped he loved me.

I'd tried to push him away but here we were. Together and it felt like the most right thing in the world. But my doubt had never been about *right now*. He could do that and had many times. What about the future? I wanted one with this man far more than I should.

Please don't break my heart, Josh.

★ ★ ★

Josh

I DIDN'T MIND mornings. I don't know that I would ever describe myself as a morning person but I'd never been the type to hit the snooze button on my alarm over and over. With a busy schedule, I always had so many things to do that lying around in bed wasn't an activity that I even contemplated all that often. I couldn't remember the last time I'd slept past seven-thirty.

With Mia next to me, however, I might just become one of those people who loll in bed all morning long.

Cuddled together like spoons, me tucked up against her back with my face buried in her fragrant reddish-gold curls, I couldn't think of one good reason to ever get out of bed. This was absolute perfection and I didn't want it to end. Soft, sweet-smelling skin. A pert bottom pressed against my morning wood. Our limbs tangled together.

A small sigh escaped from her swollen lips. Lips that had done erotic and dirty things last night. Mia might look like a little angel but she was definitely a devil between the sheets. I'd thought she might be modest or tentative but she made love with her whole heart and body.

Running my fingertip down her arm and then over the curve of her hip, I pressed light kisses to her shoulder and neck. She stirred slightly in my arms but still didn't open her eyes. Her breathing wasn't as even as before and I thought she was actually awake but pretending not to be. I knew how to get her attention.

Slipping my hand between her legs, I slowly and deliberately ran circles around her clit, ever so softly. Another sigh and then her hips began to move restlessly. Yes, she was faking. Mia wasn't asleep.

"Good morning, my princess," I whispered into her ear, snaking my tongue out to trace the shell-like curve before nibbling on the lobe. "Do you want more? Or should I stop?"

"Hmm…don't stop."

Mia still hadn't opened her eyes but that was fine. With my left hand I plucked at a rose-tipped nipple while my right continued to lavish attention on her clit. It didn't take but a few moments more and she was coming apart in my arms, her lips parted with the prettiest moans of pleasure I'd ever heard. Greedily, I wanted more. My balls were pulled up tight and my cock was aching for relief. My hunger for this woman was fierce and I didn't see any end in sight.

Reaching across her, I snagged a condom from the bedside table, making a mental note to pick up more. In our eagerness as a new couple, we were already running low.

I rolled on the condom and then lifted her right leg up and back so it rested on my own. Pressing forward, I pushed my cock into her waiting warmth. Her head fell back onto my shoulder and her teeth sunk into her full bottom lip. Sharp arrows of pleasure ran straight to my balls as her walls hugged me tightly. The pressure in my lower back was already beginning to build.

Taking my time, I pulled out and then thrust back in. Again and again, building up speed with each stroke. Mia had reached behind her and her fingers were anchored to the back of my head as I fucked her hard from behind. Her moans of pleasure urged me on along with our ragged breaths. I grunted with each thrust, my teeth gritted together painfully trying to hold back so we could come together.

"Come with me, princess. Can you do it again?"

I was hanging on by a thread, flames flowing through my veins and licking at my flesh. Mia didn't answer my hoarsely spoken question but I could barely form words and I'd hoped that I'd rendered her speechless as well.

Canting her hips at a new angle, Mia gripped my arm, her nails digging into the skin as my other hand snaked down her belly to the cleft of her thighs. Hot and inviting, it only took one, two, three rubs with my thumb and she was flying into the stars. I followed her right after, letting go all of the dammed up pleasure that I'd been desperately holding back.

We clung together for a long time afterward, our sweat-covered bodies growing cool, so I pulled the sheet up over us. It had somehow been kicked off during our morning endeavors. I dropped a kiss on her temple, filling my lungs with Mia's unique scent mixed with the musk of our lovemaking.

My only explanation is that I was happy. Really and truly happy in a way I'd never felt before. Satisfied and complete. Mia was the woman I'd been looking for and she was here in my arms. Moreover, she wanted to be there. So that's how the words popped out of my mouth. I hadn't planned it but my heart was so full. I couldn't hold them back.

"I love you, Mia."

The moment I said it I froze. The words were true but was it too soon? She'd never said the words, although she'd intimated that she'd had feelings for me for a long time. Maybe I'd just screwed everything up.

"I love you, too."

Four words. So simple. I'd heard them before from women but they'd never meant what these did.

We loved each other. Mia had given me a second chance and there was love. More than I deserved but I was going to make sure she didn't regret it.

Love didn't seem so scary anymore.

CHAPTER THIRTY-FOUR

Mia

THANKSGIVING WAS ONE of my favorite holidays. I didn't have to shop for presents and the weather was usually still pretty decent. Turkey Day kicked off the holiday season and I loved every bit of it. The decorating, the carols, the heartwarming movies on television.

And the food. Let's not forget all of the food.

Since Josh and I had been happily dating as an officially "in love" couple for the last two months our parents had decided that we all simply had to have Thanksgiving together. I'm sure they had all sorts of ideas about pushing us even closer together and dropping hints about marriage and babies. They were positively giddy that this thing between us was working out and they had about broken their own arms patting themselves on the back, all the while saying that they'd seen this coming for years. They'd known all along that we were perfect for each other.

Sure they did.

"If we're late, we're going to hear about it," I called to Josh who was still under the steamy hot water of the shower. We'd spent the night at my place, something we did more often than not. Since females needed infinitely more crap to get ready in the morning it was just easier. Besides, Josh could fall asleep on a concrete slab. He didn't care whether we were at his place or mine. He did now have a drawer plus a few shirts hanging in my closet. The bathroom had his shampoo, body wash, hair gel, razor, and shaving cream. For some reason, he simply wouldn't consent to use my pink foam that smelled of strawberries.

"I think we're going to be late, babe. Better call your mom."

"This is all your fault," I called through the half open door. Josh wasn't much for closing doors or privacy I had learned. "You kept us in bed far too late."

Having sex, of course. I'd also learned that my darling Josh had a high sex drive. We were doing it like rabbits on Red Bull, much to the delight of my sister and friends. Shelby said it was all due to her book and I just let her keep thinking that. It hadn't hurt and it had assisted me in putting my emotions to better use. Drawing a line in the sand and demanding better treatment.

What I hadn't done is set a man trap. I still hated that phrase.

"I wasn't alone in that bed. You didn't want to get out of it, either."

That was true. It was all warm and comfy under the covers. But by the time we'd levered ourselves off of the mattress we'd been horrified at the clock. I'd made a polka dot cheesecake for dessert last night but I was still expected to help cook today and it was already after noon. We would have been on the road sooner but Josh had received a business call from a software developer in London where they didn't celebrate Thanksgiving. It was just any other day there.

"Just hurry. I can practically hear my mother's voice from

here. Your mom isn't going to be too happy with you, either."

The water shut off and Josh strutted out of the shower naked as the day he was born and quite proud of it. He did, after all, have a great deal to proud of. Water rivulets slid down his tan flesh and I had the urge to lick them off one by one. But then we'd be even later than we already were. Luckily, he wrapped a towel around his waist or we wouldn't have made it to my parents' house until Christmas Eve.

"Chill, honey. They're not going to give us a hard time. They're just going to be thrilled that we're there together."

Raising my brows, I shook my head in disbelief. "I think that get out of jail free card has sailed, handsome. We can't keep using that excuse to miss Sunday dinner."

"You mixed your metaphors again." He leaned down to drop a kiss on my nose and a few droplets of water from his curls landed on my cheek. Damn, I loved his hair. If the parents were already mad... No, no, no. No more delaying. We had to leave soon. "It's so cute when you do that. Seriously, give me ten minutes and we're out of here. I just need to shave and dress."

This was a switch. Normally Josh was waiting on me. Nagging him felt so...domestic. Like we were an old married couple, which we weren't.

"I'm counting," I warned him as I left the bedroom. If I stayed we'd never leave the house. "Ten minutes."

I pulled the cheesecake from the refrigerator and made sure it was wrapped tightly for the ride to my parents. A stack of mail sat on the countertop and it had grown since Monday. I had ten minutes and it was all probably junk and bills. I could power through it and it would be one less item on my to-do list this weekend.

Junk. Junk. More junk. Electric bill. A note from my Congressman assuring me that he was voting for something I hated. This was becoming a habit with him but I shouldn't be surprised because I didn't vote for him in the first place.

A long white envelope was at the bottom of the stack and the return address had me catching my breath. The teacher exchange program had written me back and quickly, too. I hadn't expected to hear from them until more toward the end of the year.

With shaking hands and sweaty palms I ripped open the letter, sending up a plea to the universe. I really wanted to do this and it didn't have anything to do with Josh or our relationship. This had been on my list for a long time and I desperately wanted them to say yes. Closing my eyes, I steeled my spine for what might be bad news. I wouldn't be upset or cry if they didn't want me. It simply meant that this wasn't to be and I needed to find a new route to my dream. It would only be a temporary setback.

I had to read the letter several times before I could fully absorb the news. I'd been accepted. For real. There was an opening in Edinburgh, Scotland.

For January. Only a few months away. Not August as I'd originally planned. They wanted me right away and I wanted to go. There was only one small little problem.

Josh.

CHAPTER THIRTY-FIVE

Josh

INCH BY INCH, slowly but surely, I was convincing Mia that I was serious. We'd exchanged *I love yous* and I felt closer than ever to her. We were weaving each other into our regular, mundane daily lives and it was fantastic. I'd come to depend on seeing her smiling face at the beginning and end of my day. We cooked together, watched television together, laughed together, and made love together. This was far more than I'd ever imagined and I didn't know how I'd gone without it for so long.

I was in love with my best friend and it was fantastic.

I was already thinking about a real future with Mia, a commitment. It was fast but not really. We had known each other for years, after all. I was plotting a vacation after the school year was over, something warm and tropical. Moonlight, the beach, and champagne would be the perfect backdrop to propose.

And she would say yes because we were already family. The Henrys and the Kellys were having Thanksgiving together and Mia and I were the reason. Right now, the women were in the kitchen and the men were sitting in the living room watching football. A traditional arrangement that amused me but I had already been warned that the males were on cleanup duty afterward while the ladies relaxed with a glass of wine. According to my dad, I'd be elbow deep in suds before the end of the day. Honestly it seemed pretty fair.

"Mia tells me that your new game will be out next year."

The statement was from Mia's dad, Steve. I'd always thought Steve was a good guy but now that he was possibly my future father-in-law it turned our relationship completely around. I wanted him to like me. A lot. I wanted him to think that maybe I was good enough for his baby girl but that might be asking too much.

"We're in coding and unit testing right now. I'm hoping to release for summer."

Another good reason to go on vacation. The game would be out and it would be time for some rest and relaxation.

Steve chuckled. "I'm not sure what you just said but it sounds good. If I have computer problems I call Mia or Shelby to fix them."

"Mia's good with technology."

I might be biased, though. I pretty much think she's amazing.

"What do you do when the game releases?"

Luke and my dad had gone silent, apparently content to let Steve Kelly interrogate me. In fact, they'd probably put him up to it.

"Start another game project," I answered immediately. "Actually, we'll do that even before this one is released. I usually have three to four games in various stages of development at any given time."

I didn't want Steve to think that I couldn't take care of Mia or that my business wasn't self-supporting. I wasn't rolling in old family dough like Brad but I did fine. I had big plans for the future, too.

"Sounds like a lot of work. You don't do this all yourself?"

"I have a staff of thirty-five," I replied proudly. "Although most work remotely. They don't need to be in the office."

"Wouldn't that be great, Steve?" my dad laughed. "No commute. No surly co-workers or that burnt popcorn smell from the microwave. We should have picked another line of work."

My dad was an accountant. Steve worked as a supervisor at an insurance company in the claims department.

"You'd go crazy at home, Dad," Luke said.

"No, son, your mom would go crazy. She'd have planned my murder ten different ways by the end of the first week. We both need our space and my being home all day wouldn't be a good idea."

I worked from home on occasion. Would that be an issue for Mia when she was off in the summer? Would I drive her crazy and get on her nerves? It was hard to tell because we were still in that new flush of love stage where everything was fantastic with birds singing and the sun shining. And a hell of a lot of sex. I'm pretty sure our parents knew why we were late today because my mom gave me the side eye when we got here.

"There are some days I'd love to work from home," my brother said, shooting me a meaningful glance.

"Then you should do it," I said. "You know...for someone else."

Steve and my dad seemed to think that was funny, both chuckling at the jabs between brothers.

"Kids," my dad laughed. "They love to torture each other. My boys do it and I bet your girls do, too."

"They do," Steve replied with a grin. "But it's more subtle. They'll understand when they have their own."

"I wouldn't mind a grandchild or two," my dad said loudly, looking back and forth between me and Luke. "Any day would be fine. I don't want to be too old to enjoy them."

"That's right, Luke. Better get on that," I said, elbowing my brother. "What are you and Rachel waiting for?"

"You're the oldest. I'm waiting on you."

Steve's expression turned serious and for the first time that day I could definitely see that he was sizing me up. "What about you, Josh? Do you want kids someday?"

"Yes, sir. I do."

"But you're not in a hurry."

It was a statement, not a question. So technically, I could say nothing but I kind of got the feeling that he and the others expected me to respond.

"I think it's more up to the female than the male. After all, her life is thrown into chaos. She should probably make the final decision."

I'd apparently answered correctly because Steve smiled. "That's true but don't underestimate just how much your life will change, son. Everything will be different. Mark my words."

I was ready for different.

Mia

THE NEXT DAY I went Black Friday shopping with the girls. I wasn't much into the whole shop till you drop mentality but luckily none of us really cared if we bought anything. It was more about just getting together, eating lunch, and swapping Thanksgiving stories. We ended up at a restaurant a few miles from the mall but it was still busy with patrons enjoying the long weekend.

We were halfway through our entrees when there was a lull in the conversation. The time had come.

"I heard from the teacher exchange program. I was accepted."

Everyone started talking at once, loud and excited, until Ashlyn placed her hands over her ears. "Can we keep it down? People are starting to look."

Shelby glanced around the room and grimaced. "Sorry. I'm just excited. This is so cool. Where would you go?"

"Scotland."

Clapping her hands together, Emmy smiled. "I have always wanted to visit Scotland. I am definitely coming out to see you."

"Start from the beginning," Ashlyn said. "You opened this in your mail this morning… Tell us everything."

As succinctly as possible, I outlined the details. Where I would be going and when. The fact was I didn't have all that much information and wouldn't until I accepted the exchange.

"You haven't accepted it yet?" Ashlyn asked, a frown on her face. "But you're going to, right?"

"There's no one in the office to take my call. It's a holiday," I pointed out. "And yes, I'm pretty sure that I'm going to accept it."

"Pretty sure," Emmy echoed. "But not completely sure?"

"I want to go. It's just…"

"Josh," Emmy finished for me. "What did he say? Was he an asshole?"

"I haven't told him yet."

All three women went silent. This was a first. None of my friends knew what to say. I'll write this down in my diary.

"No advice? I'm disappointed in you most of all, Shelby. You live for this shit."

"I'm still trying to process that you'll be gone during all of the wedding preparations. I thought you were going to be there for me."

"You get one day," Ashlyn said, holding up one finger. "One. You're not a princess. You don't even play one on TV."

"You are not the center of the universe, sunshine," Emmy said with an evil smile. "Not even close. You cannot ask your sister to stay here because you need her to pick out wedding crap. Geez, have you heard of the internet? She can do it from Scotland."

"I said I was processing it," Shelby replied crisply. "I didn't say that she shouldn't go."

"So you think she should go?" Emmy pressed.

"You should go," Shelby said, turning back to me. "This is an amazing opportunity for you and you'd be crazy to pass it up."

She was saying words I wanted to hear but did she mean

them? I wanted to go but not at the expense of alienating my only sister.

"What about the wedding planning?"

Shelby shot Emmy a look. "As I've been reminded we're pretty much done. We've done so much the last two months that the only thing left is the wedding favors and Emmy and Ashlyn can help me with that. The dress, the venue, the band, the cake, even the photographer is all set. You've been more help than I ever could have imagined, especially since Brad was no help at all. I'm just going to miss you, that's all. I kind of like having you around."

"What have you done with my sister?" I asked Emmy. "It's almost like she's being reasonable."

Shelby rolled her eyes and Emmy laughed so hard she had to hold her ribs. "She normally is when she isn't thinking about four-tiered cakes."

"Apparently I'm not the center of the universe," Shelby said in a tart tone. "That was a huge letdown for me."

"I'll bet it was. Now that I've told you, I still have to tell Josh."

All the smiles disappeared, replaced with far more sober expressions.

"What do you think he'll do?" Ashlyn asked. "If he asks you to stay, will you do it?"

"I've been asking myself that same question since yesterday morning," I confessed. "I want to go but I want Josh, too. I'm just not sure that I can have both of them."

"It's not forever," Shelby declared. "He could come visit. He owns his own business, for heaven's sake. It's not like he doesn't have the vacation time or the money. He's all modest but his company is extremely successful."

I'd had the same thought. I'd love for the two of us to explore the country together.

"I don't think he's ever compromised for anyone before," I said, my heart heavy and my appetite gone. "He's always put his career before anything. Or anyone."

"You want him to put you first," Ashlyn said.

"Yes, but maybe that's not realistic. Maybe that's too much to ask for."

"No," Emmy said firmly. "It is not, so get that idea out of your head once and for all. Of course, it's not too much. You said it yourself…you deserve better."

That's what I believed. But as a child I'd believed in unicorns too, and that hadn't turned out well.

"I want him and the trip."

Ashlyn signaled the waitress. "First, we need to toast your acceptance. Then we need to think about this. You two have been really happy lately. I mean disgustingly so, like making everybody around you want to gag. Surely, Josh loves you enough to want to support you in this."

"I want to trust him," I replied slowly. "I want to believe that he will, it's just that I've seen him walk away from relationship after relationship, and for dumb stuff, too. He always had a reason but it didn't always make much sense. This might just be the reason to end things that he's been looking for."

"You had Thanksgiving dinner with him and his family yesterday," Emmy reasoned. "That's not a man looking for an escape chute. It's a man shopping for engagement rings."

"I seriously doubt that."

Josh had never mentioned marriage much in all the years I'd known him except on the rare occasion that he'd be asked about it. Then he usually made a joke about not being in any hurry. I wasn't in a hurry either, but lately I'd begun to think that it might be nice. Someday down the road. That might just be the hopeless romantic in me, though.

"I see it every day," Emmy insisted. "Every single day. He's a man in love."

I didn't doubt our love. I could see and feel it as if it was a tangible thing.

Shelby placed her fork on the edge of her plate. "Mia, you are not bound by any promises you made while having a gun pointed at your heart. I get that you have this new outlook on life but it's okay if you decide that you don't want to go to Scotland. It's okay if you want to stay here. No one will think any less of you."

"That's not it," I said, shaking my head. "I do want to go. That moment did change me and I can't go back to who I was before. I can't go back to waiting for my life to happen, being passive. I'm happy that I've changed, but it's not always easy. It's hard not to slide into old habits that weren't good for me."

My sister smiled and reached across the table to grab my hand, giving it a reassuring squeeze. "Then you have your answer."

I did, although I'd made it as difficult as possible to get there. I wanted this, and if Josh wanted me he had to want the person that I had become. I had to gather my strength and extend trust to the man I loved.

I was worth waiting for. I was worth being placed first every now and then. The only open question was if I'd fallen in love with a man that could do that.

All those years of loving Josh had come down to this.

CHAPTER THIRTY-SIX

Josh

"**D**ID YOU HAVE fun with the girls today?" I asked Mia when she showed up at my house for dinner. We'd planned to just order in and have a quiet night.

While I had toiled at the office, she'd spent the day with her friends shopping. I'd texted her a few times but hadn't heard much. They must have been having a great time, although Mia only had a few bags. Was there something in there for me? She'd been hinting around all week without coming right out and asking me what I wanted for Christmas.

"It was exhausting. So many people. The mall was a zoo. We ended up eating lunch and talking."

I waggled my eyebrows playfully. "Did you get me anything?"

"You're worse than a kid," Mia scolded, shaking a finger at me. "You can bet that I'm hiding your gift until the last minute. I know that you snoop."

I did snoop. I loved the excitement and the surprises but my curiosity always got the better of me. The next thing I knew I was digging in closets for hidden gifts. I'm not proud of it...

"I'm going to pour myself a glass of wine. Do you want a

beer?"

"That sounds good. I worked on finalizing the storyboard today. It's officially in the next phase of the project."

Mia handed me a cold bottle and then sat down at the kitchen island, her expression somber. "That's wonderful. I'm so happy for you. It's going to be a great success."

"I'd believe you except that you look like your hamster died. Where's that smile I love so much? Is something wrong?"

Perhaps she and Shelby had butted heads again. From what I'd been hearing, the future bride was becoming a pain in the ass. Very unShelby-like.

Mia took a sip of her wine and then shook her head. "Actually, I have good news, too. I heard from the teacher exchange program. They've accepted me."

Elated at the news, I zipped around the corner of the island and pulled her into a hug before pressing a kiss to those tempting lips. She tasted like wine and the mint in her lip gloss. "Baby, that's amazing. You must be so excited."

Or she should be. This was something she'd wanted and now she was getting it. But she wasn't happy and smiling like she should be.

"Did they offer you a terrible destination?" I asked, sliding onto the bar stool next to hers. "Do they want to send you to a place where it's snowing all year long?"

Intently studying her glass, she wouldn't look at me. Not a good sign. A bar of dread began to build in my gut. "It's Scotland, actually. And I'd leave in January."

January. The word hung in the air for a long moment, slowly penetrating my brain. January. That wasn't that far away. Just a little over a month. I'd been prepared for September but this was something of a surprise.

"This January?"

"Yes." She finally looked up, our gazes clashing. "I want to accept it, Josh."

Of course, she did. That's what all of this was about. I just wasn't quite prepared for her to go so soon but I'd better get my shit together. "You should. Accept it, I mean."

Did she think I was going to ask her to stay? I was a bastard but not that kind of bastard. We'd work it out somehow. This was what she'd wanted and I'd be a jerk to try and stop her.

"I'll be gone through July."

"I assumed that."

Something was going on here. I could hear the warning bells in my skull but I didn't know exactly what was happening inside of that beautiful head of hers.

"So I would understand if you don't want to continue this. I understand that you may not want to wait."

What was she talking about? Was she breaking up with me? No, she thought I was going to break up with her. She didn't have a clue.

I loved Mia but there were times I had no idea how her mind worked. She'd twisted all of this up into a tangled mess, and she was beginning to piss me off. My grip on the beer bottle tightened as I gritted my teeth. What in the fuck was happening here?

"You're okay with us ending things?"

Her eyes widened and she took another drink of her wine. Apparently, she needed the alcohol. I – on the other hand – was stone cold sober and getting angrier by the second. She didn't know what she thought she knew.

"Well...obviously I'm not happy about it, but I get that seven months is a long time." Her little chin lifted and her expression became almost defiant. "I've wanted to do this for a long time and I can't pass up this opportunity, Josh. Not even for you."

Christ on a cracker, she'd actually thought I would tell her not to go. I didn't like her lack of trust in me. Not one bit.

Reining in my anger, I took a deep calming breath. Yelling wasn't going to get us anywhere.

"I'm not happy with you, Mia."

"I know–"

"You don't know shit," I interrupted. "I'm not upset because you've decided to accept the invitation. I'm happy for you. Of course, I'm upset because you'll be gone. That's a no brainer, baby. But I'm more upset that you didn't trust me. You automatically went straight to the worst-case scenario. That we're over. You don't believe in me, or us."

The old Mia would have stayed calm and accepted my critique. But this new feisty Mia wasn't going to take any of my crap. Damn, I loved her. Her cheeks were red and her green eyes practically shot sparks at me. Slapping her hand on the table, Mia moved closer to me so that we were almost nose to nose. "I did so believe in us. I believed in you. I sure as hell hoped you loved me enough and that's why I told you. If I didn't believe in us I would have quietly turned down the invitation and said nothing to you. You never would have known and I would have stayed here like a good little girl. But I didn't do that. Asshole."

I didn't know whether to laugh or yell. She'd called me an asshole. So naturally, too. How often had she called me that when I wasn't around? Because it sure slid off her tongue easily. "Did you actually think about not going? And I'm not an asshole."

"Yes," she said, her eyes glittering with unshed tears. "I did. But I also knew that I couldn't change the person that I've become for you. And sometimes you can be an asshole."

I couldn't argue that point. My friends and family wouldn't argue it, either.

I deserve better.

I remembered her saying it. Now she was living it, which made me proud. It still hurt, however, that she'd thought I might not be supportive.

"What made you think I wouldn't be happy for you? That we couldn't work this out?"

For a moment I didn't think she was going to answer. She'd turned away and slid off of the barstool, walking over to the windows. Finally she looked back, her cheeks damp with tears. Shit, I'd made her cry. I really was an asshole.

"You've never been the kind of guy that was in for the long haul with a woman. You've always put your work first and relationships second."

I wanted to tell her that she was wrong but she wasn't. I wanted to tell her that she was being delusional but she'd pretty much nailed it. I wasn't the man that women could depend on when the going got rough. That's when I usually made my exit… If we ever got there to begin with.

I'd been trying to show Mia that she was different but two

months wasn't the longest time. Clearly it hadn't been enough to show her I'd changed.

My anger slowly ebbed away. What a fucking mess this was. I was proud of Mia. She'd stood up for what she'd wanted but the fact that she'd thought she might have to choose between me and her dreams was sad. I would never make her do that.

Words were cheap. She needed actions to show her how I felt.

Slowly, so as not to spook her, I moved until we were close enough that I could feel the heat from her body and smell the delicious scent that was all Mia. She was looking up at me, obviously still on edge. Her shoulders were rigid and her lips trembling but I could see the love and hope she couldn't hide.

"When a man's in love, he wants his woman to have everything she's dreamed of. He doesn't want to stand in the way of those dreams. I love you. Do you love me?"

★   ★   ★

Mia

OF COURSE, I loved him. This wouldn't be difficult if I didn't.

"I love you. You know that."

With a fingertip, he traced the curve of my jaw. Just his touch had me melting, and I closed my eyes to savor the sensation. My knees turned to jelly and I had to grip the wall to keep from falling in a heap at his feet.

"I know that I haven't given you many reasons to trust that I'm sticking around but please believe me when I say that spending the rest of my life with you is what's most important to me. Did you know that I was already planning a beach vacation for the two of us when school ends?"

Opening my eyes, his soft blue gaze was filled with love and adoration. "I didn't know that."

"You probably also didn't know that I was planning on proposing then, too."

I sucked in a shocked breath, searching his expression for any sign of joking. Was he serious? He wanted to marry me? Holy shit.

"I'm totally serious," he said, reading my mind perfectly. "I was planning it. I guess now I'll have to do it in Scotland."

My brain was still back on the whole proposal thing.

"Scotland?"

His smiled gently, his thumb caressing my lips. "I know that this is important to you. So I guess I'll just have to tag along."

"Tag along?"

I'd officially become a parrot but my mind was mush. He wanted to marry me. He wanted to have a real future with me. He wanted to go to Scotland.

"I have my own business. I can work from anywhere. I may not be able to stay in Scotland the entire seven months but I think I can spend most of my time there and just come back here when I need to."

The fear and dread I'd felt when this conversation first started had fallen away. No, it had been pushed out by the most wonderful feeling of joy I'd ever experienced. A thousand butterflies had been set free in my abdomen and their wings tickled my ribs, making me laugh and smile. This man…I was speechless.

Almost. Let's face it. I like to talk.

"That's a huge compromise for me. Are you sure?"

"It's for us, my sweet Mia. Us." He chuckled and shook his head. "You're not getting this. I love you. We as a couple come first. It's good practice for when we get married and have a family. We'll go to Scotland. Together. We'll make it work. Together. You were ready to walk away and that scares me but at the same time I'm busting my buttons with pride. You said that you deserved more and that you wouldn't settle for anything less. Let me be the man to give it to you and hold me to the highest standards. I might need a little practice, but I'll get there."

My vision was blurred and it took a moment for me to realize that I was crying. Not from sadness but from sheer unadulterated happiness. I could have Josh and my dreams, too. I'd expected better but what I'd received was...

More. Far more than I'd ever imagined. It wouldn't be easy. We'd disagree, argue, make up, and then find a compromise. We'd make plans for the future as best we could and we'd struggle to balance it all. But he was right that we'd do it together. We were far stronger as a couple than we were apart. He'd shown me that I could trust him with my heart and now he owned it completely. I had his as well.

Josh's love was better than any fantasy I'd had as a girl growing up. This was real. Our future held so many possibilities I couldn't wait for it to start.

Together.

I made a mental note to thank my sister. She'd written that silly man trap book after all, and it had helped me not settle for less. Shelby would probably be insufferable now but she deserved a few kudos.

Grabbing the front of Josh's t-shirt I pulled him closer, a teasing smile on my face. "This is where you kiss me to seal the deal."

Chuckling, he leaned down, a few curls falling over his forehead. "That sounds like an excellent start, but I think your plan needs work."

I was open to suggestions.

"I'm listening."

His lips pressed against mine and for a few minutes the world melted away and there was no one else in the universe but the two of us. When he finally lifted his head, the bastard had a grin a mile wide. He knew he was good. I, on the other hand, was a mess. Ragged breathing, hot cheeks, and a simmering warmth flying through my veins.

"I say we seal the deal in a more personal way," he said with a naughty glint in his eye. "Preferably naked."

"I like the sound of that. The naked part, too."

We left a trail of clothes all the way to the bedroom.

I hope you enjoyed Josh and Mia's story! There will be more in the Man Trap series coming soon.

Thank you for reading Tempt Him.

Don't miss a thing! Sign up to be notified of Olivia's new releases:

Mailing List

oliviajaymesoptin.instapage.com

About The Author

Olivia Jaymes is a wife, mother, lover of sexy romance, and caffeine addict. She lives with her husband and son in central Florida and spends her days with handsome alpha males and spunky heroines.

She is currently working on a new contemporary romance series – *Man Trap* in addition to her other ongoing series.

Visit Olivia Jaymes at
www.OliviaJaymes.com

Other Titles by Olivia Jaymes

Danger Incorporated

Damsel In Danger

Hiding From Danger

Discarded Heart Novella

Indecent Danger

Embracing Danger

Danger In The Night

Reunited With Danger

Window to Danger

Road to Danger

Cowboy Justice Association

Cowboy Command

Justice Healed

Cowboy Truth

Cowboy Famous

Cowboy Cool

Imperfect Justice

The Deputies

Justice Inked

Justice Reborn

Vengeful Justice

Justice Divided

Military Moguls
Champagne and Bullets
Diamonds and Revolvers
Caviar and Covert Ops
Emeralds, Rubies, and Camouflage

Midnight Blue Beach
Wicked After Midnight
Midnight Of No Return
Kiss Midnight Goodbye

The Hollywood Showmance Chronicles
A Kiss For the Cameras
Swinging From A Star
Wild on the Red Carpet
Love in the Spotlight
And the Winner is